Condemned Courier

Cindy Koepp

Lumen Anime
Citron Concassé
Aberdeen, Washington, USA

Condemned Courier

PRINTING HISTORY
First Edition
June 2018

ISBN-10: 0999592731
ISBN-13: 978-0-9995927-3-1

CREDITS
Cover Art by: Matt Ostrom

PUBLISHER'S NOTE

Condemned Courier

Prologue

Karl sat in the corner of the house by the side of the hearth where no one would find him. If they didn't find him, he wouldn't have to go. He could stay in his own house. Papa, Mama, Bridget, and Volker were already done moving things out. They could finish in the barn and the shed, and leave if they wanted to. He sniffled and wiped his eyes on his sleeve.

The front door creaked open. Karl hugged his knees to his chest and tried to disappear behind the corner of the hearth.

"Karl?" Mama called.

He clenched his jaw and squeezed his eyes closed. Tears ran down his cheeks. The sound of Mama's footsteps came closer.

Her skirts rustled just in front of him, and her warm hand stroked his cheek. "It's time to go, Karl."

He looked up at her and tensed so hard he shook. "*Nein!* It's our house! Ours! Why do we have to go?"

"Because our king made a treaty with the Aelstrian king. We have to move to our side of the river."

"I want to stay here, Mama!"

"*Ja, mein Schatz*, and I dearly wish we could, but we cannot." She offered Karl her hand. "We must go. Giving up our house means your father and

Volker do not have to go to war. They can stay home and be a father and a brother to you. Do you agree that is better, or is a house worth more than your father and brother?"

Karl dried his eyes on his sleeve and accepted Mama's hand up. "It's not fair, Mama."

"I know, but it is right. We are on the wrong side of the river. It is not the Aelstrians' fault. We have somewhere to live and neighbors to help us. All will be well, *mein Schatz*. All will be well."

He clung to Mama and followed her outside. The wagon with all their things was packed up, tied down, and hitched to the horses. Papa led the horses. Bridget carried two cages, each with a chicken in it. Volker kept the sheep together with a little help from the dog. Mama unwrapped a rope from a post by the door and gave it a tug. Karl followed it back to their milk cow at the other end. He clutched Mama's hand and walked with her, taking two steps to each of hers.

They walked the whole morning before reaching the bridge over the Heiligstrom River. The stone bridge connected the two parts of the land Karl's family owned. Until today, the other side was for farming. Now it would be where they and the animals lived, too.

A tan-feathered Aelstrian stood next to the bridge. Karl used to think Aelstrians were fun to watch. They looked just like a big bird, but with hands on the ends of their wings and long, thin feathers streaming behind their heads. Karl had never seen one fly, but he'd always wanted to meet one. Now that he had the chance, he wished there had never been any Aelstrians on the whole world. Then maybe the dumb kings wouldn't have made a treaty to make them leave home.

The Aelstrian waiting by the bridge wore a brilliant blue tunic that had no sleeves. Sparkly beads decorated the long feathers on his head. Papa slowed as they neared the bridge.

"I have the word of the king, *Herr* Schild'ann," The Aelstrian tucked his beak to his chest and fluffed the feathers on the back of his head.

"I'm listening," Papa said, his voice much calmer than Karl felt.

"The words of the king. 'This is a sad event. Relocating a nest is difficult, and I honor the sacrifice you give to avert hostilities. I know that nothing I could offer is truly worthy of your sacrifice. Still it is the wish of these feathers that you will receive this gift.'" The Aelstrian offered Papa a black pouch with swirls embroidered into it.

Papa tugged the pouch open and peeked inside. His eyes widened. "This is most generous. More than we paid for the land in the first place. Please express my gratitude to the king."

"I will." The Aelstrian tucked his beak to his chest for a moment then walked away. As he passed Karl, he paused. His wings drooped a little. "These feathers grieve for you, fledgling. Taking a fledgling out of the nest too soon is a sad thing. The light in the sky, however, is that fledglings adapt easiest of us all. You are sad today, and with good reason. The sun will shine for you soon." He tucked his beak to his chest then continued on his way.

Papa tied the pouch to his belt and urged the

horses across the bridge.

"What was it, Ernst? What's in the bag?" Mama asked.

Papa clasped her hand. "I'll show you when we get home."

Karl glanced back toward their old house, hoping for a moment that they would be turning around, but Papa kept leading them along the path edging the farmland. The land on this side had more hills but fewer rocks. The crops were up to Karl's knees already. By his birthday, some of them would be taller than him, just like last year.

At the top of the hill, Mama pointed to a stone and wood house, different from the old house but bigger. "There's our new house."

Karl's jaw dropped. "That's ours? Where did it come from?"

Volker snorted. "From the sky, of course."

"Be nice." Mama glared at him. "He's been with me the whole time you and Papa have been working on it."

Karl looked up at Mama. "Papa and Volker built it?"

"*Ja,* with help from the neighbors."

The new house was on the top of a hill near the river but not right on it. Several wagons and horses were waiting outside a small fence around the house, a little barn, and a shed. As Papa brought the cart up to the gate, the door of the house opened, and all the papas and big boys from the neighbors all around them—some from really far away—rushed out. Some helped Volker get the sheep into the barn. Two took the chickens from Bridget and let them loose in the yard. The rest helped Papa untie the ropes around the wagon. Each took something from the wagon and brought it inside. Karl followed Mama and Bridget around to the back of the house and in through a second door. They entered the kitchen where all the mamas and girls from the neighbors were setting out food on the big table.

Mama leaned over and kissed Karl's forehead. "Go play now, but stay inside the fence."

Karl walked outside and leaned on the fence. Maybe, if he stared hard enough, he could see his home.

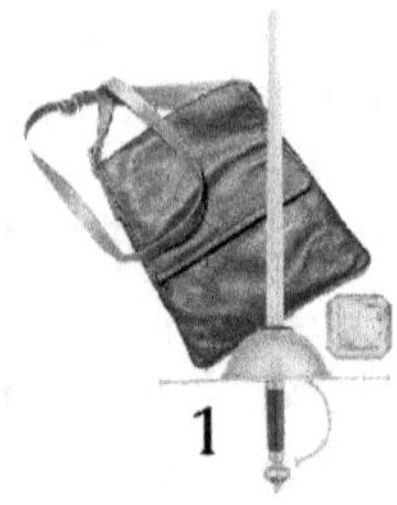

1

Crown Prince Evryt Lixine stood and gazed out the window with a view of the tree canopy. Brilliantly colored glass ornaments hanging from the branches swayed in the early spring breeze. The trees were blooming all around, with very few full leaves, but the servants had already exchanged the icicles and snowflakes for the spring butterflies and flowers. The glass ornaments caught the sunlight that found its way through the canopy and created colored splotches like a child's kaleidoscope.

One of the colored dots swept across Evryt's scaly hand, feathered arm, and the towels still tucked around the window frame to ward off the morning chill. A fire burned in the fireplace, giving off light, heat, and the gentle background noise that Father liked so much.

Father roosted on a soft bed. A blue canopy and curtains were closed on all but one side, keeping in the warmth. A beautiful quilt covered Father up to the base of his neck, and his head rested on an embroidered pillow. He slept so much of the day now. A few hours of wakefulness in the afternoon were all anyone could hope for. Even mealtimes had become sporadic.

He groaned in his sleep.

Evryt sat next to his father's bed and preened the

thin feathers above his ear holes. The bedclothes disguised how frail and thin Father had become over the last few months, but skin and feathers sagged on his head. Illness during his last molt had marred all his feathers leaving pale, weakened stripes.

Father's shallow breathing wheezed more loudly. He opened his eyes and turned his head toward Evryt. "Evryt? Still here? No sense hanging around here, lad. You have a wife to attend to."

"She understands my choice," Evryt whistled.

Father slid one wing out of the blankets and patted Evryt's hand. "Evryt, listen."

He leaned closer, pushing the royal blue curtain further aside. "I'm here, Father."

"Evryt, you have to fix what's wrong in the court. I couldn't do it myself. There weren't any good alternatives, but you have to fix it. Restore the proper line on the throne. Find and deal with the corrupt nobles. I'm sorry, lad. I couldn't leave you a better legacy."

This again. "I know, Fa–"

"It's not fair, not to you or Jianna." Father's grip tightened. "You would make a good king. I know you would, but you can't. Civil war is coming on wind-driven wings. You have to restore the proper line, but not Yarek. Don't abdicate to Yarek, or instead of civil war, it will be a war to exterminate the humans."

"I understand." Evryt preened Father's feathers, and a few came loose in his fingers. "I'll find a way to restore the proper heir on the throne. I promise. I've already talked to Jianna, and she understands, too. She says she didn't marry me to be queen."

"I should have done it myself. I should have

found a way."

"I'll set things right. Yarek will make a mistake or die of old age, and I'll abdicate to the proper heir. I promise. I'll set things right just like we talked about." Evryt scooted his chair closer. "Just rest, Father. I'll fix everything as soon as I can."

Father nodded and tucked his weathered beak under his pale gray wing. His breathing wheezed through his nares and settled into a slower rhythm for sleep. Evryt was still there preening his father's soft, worn feathers when the king flew on to a greater nest.

Royal Courier Addya Dace stood at the edge of the gathering. The former king was laid out on a low platform of treated wood. His favorite silver and blue tunic glittered in the sunset. The morticians' efforts showed the king peaceful now, not the sickly, elderly bird he had been for the last few months. The Soon-to-Be-King, Evryt, cast a fistful of fire coloring onto his father's body before using a torch to ignite the wood. The fire spread quickly, casting off a brilliant wall of flame the same orange as the sunset, and the same blue as the late king's tunic.

He whistled the *Song of Farewell*. As the immediate heir, the first verse was his alone. Then on the next, other family members joined, and on the last everyone participated, each taking the descants or harmonies as fit their moods and talents.

On the final note, Addya reached for the highest in the chord, a personal honor she saved only for those worthy Aelstrians who impressed her with their integrity and honor.

The final note ended on the proper count, except for a few stragglers who missed the cutoff. After a few moments of silence, Evryt led Jianna away. Once they were gone, everyone else filed out. Addya stayed still, in part to spend a few last moments with her former king and in part to let the crowds clear the walkway. All that jostling and bumping would give her bruised toes and mangled tail feathers.

"So what do you think of our new king?" one tan-feathered female muttered.

Addya clenched her beak to keep from scolding the female. *Quiet! Or I'll give your beak such a whack!*

"That one? He's barely out of pinfeathers!" the tan female's companion said. "Might as well put an egg on the throne."

Better to have someone older and incompetent? Evryt can do this. He is young, but he's no fool. Now shut that beak!

The two gossipers passed out of range.

Other murmurs reached her, but she rarely heard more than the occasional syllable. She managed to catch the eye of one of the offenders, a lesser count named Pisa, and communicated the proper etiquette with her narrow-eyed glare. To Pisa's credit, he quit talking and elbowed his equally offensive companion.

Once everyone had left, Addya walked over to the pyre, stopping a couple arm-lengths away. The fire warmed her gray feathers and blue tunic. Kneeling, she touched her beak to her chest and fluffed out her head feathers for the old king, giving him the respect he'd earned throughout his life, all the way to the end. Finally, she stood and strode down the walkway.

Evryt entered the room where all seven of the landed nobility were gathered. Count Zyrus Quetik, very nearly Father's age, had naturally black plumage edged with the gray of years. The droopy skin around his eyes gave him the appearance of weariness. His heavy green and gold brocade tunic suggested that at his age, he was having trouble keeping warm. He'd chosen the seat nearest the fireplace.

Next to him, Duke Dartin Lixine, father's half-brother, perched with his tail feathers perilously close to the fireplace. A couple feathers on one edge of his tail were frayed. In fact, many of his brown and black feathers were in some disarray.

On Quetik's other side, Countess Fallie Jadan sat picking loose bits of lint and down feathers from her brilliant, yellow velvet gown. Her crest was thoroughly ornamented, more gold-beaded chains than feathers. She wouldn't be the first hen to trim her crest back just enough to clip the gleaming chains to the shafts of her feathers.

Across from her was the current, proper heir to

the throne. So many years ago, Great Grandfather had disinherited his eldest and passed the throne to Evryt's grandfather. Stopping the war with the humans was more vital than securing the proper royal line. Full of the knowledge of her true station, the Countess Talia Yarek had perched her excessive bulk across two chairs.

Count Gado Azel sat sideways, mangling tail feathers on the arm of his chair. His solid brown wing feathers and tail feathers were bent in haphazard directions. Other feathers, too, were damaged and out of place. The count was in dire need of a good preening.

The last two were the brothers. Except that they'd hatched three days apart, they might have been twins. One had inherited the hen's territory and the other the father's. Rach and Orak Anat were identical all the way to the streak of black across the cream-colored feathers on their heads. Only the color of their tunics could distinguish them.

As Evryt found his place, he searched the observation gallery above. His beloved Jianna sat watching, and next to her, the new head of his couriers. The two of them here would make this difficult meeting manageable. They wouldn't be able to speak out, nor would protocol allow them to do more than simply observe, but just having them present quieted some of the tension across his back and chest.

He sat on his padded stool and regarded his nobility. "Thank you for coming to bid my father farewell. I know how hard it is to leave your flock for even a short time, and for some of you, coming to the capital is a significant journey."

Yarek tipped her head to one side and narrowed her eyes. "Dispense with the formal frippery, and let's get to task. We all know that your father intended to restore the proper royal line, and I think it–"

Evryt held up a hand to stall the countess. "Yes, and he gave me clear suggestions of how and when that transfer should occur."

"And?" Yarek studied her fingernails.

"It will not happen as long as you're alive to take the throne!" Quetik pounded one fist into the other palm.

Yarek hissed. "Close your weathered beak, you old corpse."

"Oh, no, he's quite right." Jadan sat forward and ruffled her tail feathers. "Putting you on the throne would undo the whole reason why your line is not on the throne now. You would no sooner be crowned than the war with Schafland would start again."

Azel leaned closer to Yarek. "Why do you want a war with the humans?"

She pushed him away. "Because, you buffoon, the humans are worthless creatures taking up space that should be ours."

Evryt's stomach soured, but when he opened his beak to speak, Quetik cut him off.

"So never mind the treaty signed in good faith and the pledges the king gave to the displaced humans."

The duke snorted. "Pledges? How long are we expected to honor the promises of a dead king?"

"No, not a dead king." Evryt shook his head and

pointed at the duke. "Those pledges were from the crown, not simply the king. As long as there's a crown, the pledges should be honored."

"The humans have done nothing to instigate hostilities," Quetik insisted.

Azel tapped Yarek's wing. "I don't think I like humans. Dad never did."

"With cause." She hissed in disgust and turned away from him. "You're too young to be king, Evryt."

"And still he will be!" For such an old bird, Quetik still managed to jump to his feet and jabbed his finger at Yarek.

Rach glanced at his brother and hissed. "For now. War with the humans would be a bad idea. They have developed newer, better weapons. We still have superiority in the air, but going to war with them would be stupid. We could lose our route to the ocean and our ports."

"Exactly." Orak rested a hand on Rach's shoulder. "So, no, Countess, we will not support your claim to the throne, but if a better heir is not placed on the throne soon, we might reconsider, Your Highness."

Evryt clenched his beak hard. *Really? And I suppose you think that I'm so young you could just push me around?*

Jadan leaned forward. "No one will displace the king without reprisal, Orak. Hear me."

And so would begin a civil war. Quetik and Jadan with me. All others against for their own reasons.

"And what of my claim to the throne?" the duke asked.

Quetik shook his head. "Wrong family line."

"No less wrong than his!" The duke glared at Evryt and clicked his beak.

Thanks, Uncle. "We would get no closer to the correct house on the throne with a trade between you and me."

"Actually, trading the duke for the prince would put us further from the proper family line, so no. We wouldn't support that." Rach propped both hands on his hips and waggled his elbows to rustle his wings.

Yarek huffed. "You would support a fledgling before you would support experience?"

Evryt squinted at the fat old bird. "I'm not that much younger than my father was when he ascended to the throne."

"I am in the correct house for the throne. You are not!" Yarek wobbled to her feet and fell back onto the stools, one of which creaked ominously. "I live in the proper capital. You do not!"

Quetik ruffled all his feathers on end and lifted his wings. "You would break a treaty and send us into a war we probably could not win. He would not!"

"It's no good, Countess," Rach said.

Orak absently preened his cheek feathers. "The prince may not be in the right line, and he's younger than any king in history, but he's closer to the proper line than the duke and not at all likely to send us into a hopeless war."

After a good long hiss, directed at all of them, Yarek struggled to her feet and stomped out the door, shaking the floor and everything in the room on the way.

Azel looked around with sudden twists of his head. "Oh, are we finished already? Dad always said these meetings took forever." He launched himself to his feet, landed on one foot badly off-balanced, and fell toward the fire. "Oops!"

Jadan caught him across the chest inches away from the hearth. "Take care, Count."

"Thanks."

The duke paused on his way past. "You'd best reconsider."

Evryt stood taller and stared down at his uncle. "You'd best remember your place, sir. I am crown prince until tomorrow's coronation."

On the way out the door, the duke hissed.

The brothers rose and stepped over.

"We support you," Rach said.

"For now." Orak's eyes narrowed.

Evryt blew out a breath. "I understand. I really do have plans to honor my father's wishes as soon as a proper heir is in position."

The pair left together as Jadan walked over. "You have my support, Prince. Do not disappoint me."

Before he could answer she left and Quetik rose. "I have confidence in you, lad."

I'm glad someone does. "Thank you."

As the old count left, Evryt crouched next to the fire and stared at the flames

2

Addya walked around her class as they did their parry drills, correcting form and footwork as necessary. She kept a mental list of the ones who were clearly in the wrong class, either too high or too low.

A loud hiss and a clatter of metal on wood drew her attention to the far side of the room. Uri, a new but older student, muttered as he walked in a tight circle and rubbed his shoulder. The other four pairs abruptly stopped their drills and scrambled back.

Addya slipped through the rank of students and approached Uri and his partner. She checked Uri's practice armor for damage. *What is it this time, O whiner extraordinaire?* "No blood, so it can't be as bad as all that. Explanation?"

Uri hissed. "This is a complete waste of time! All we do is practice parries, practice point control, practice footwork. When will we learn how to fight?"

"You are learning how to fight. What do you think fighting is composed of? Hm? Blade control, footwork, attacks, and parries." *But that's not what you want. You want to leap forward into mastery right away.* "When you first learned to speak, did you launch off into full-fledged sentences or did you first learn the sounds?"

He leaned closer and fluffed out his feathers. "I

know all this. We've been doing nothing else for weeks."

"Apparently not if you're still missing basic parries." She pointed to his shoulder. "Pair up again, fledglings, and continue the drill with your opposite hand."

Four and a half groups paired up for another round of practice, but Uri stomped closer and propped his hands on his hips. All his feathers fluffed forward. "No. I want to prove I can move up to the next class."

Addya picked up his practice blade and handed it to him then pointed to his waiting partner. "Your partner is there. Parry drills. Off hand."

He hissed. "I want to prove to you I'm ready!"

"Then you will not continue the lesson?"

"No."

She walked over to the lockbox where she kept the students' payments for class. After counting out the cost of half a day's fee, she returned to Uri and handed him the money. She took the practice blade from him. "I'm sorry to hear that. You were a student with great potential."

"But—" Uri hefted the coins in his hand then offered them to Addya.

She lined up with his former partner, switched the blade to her off hand and nodded once. Her student made a thrust for her chest. She parried and returned the attempt at half-speed. His parry was a little late but effective. They continued the pattern.

"Wait a minute. I don't want to go." Uri offered her the money again.

"Then you should resume your place here so I

can observe and correct the class as needed."

His eyes narrowed. "That's not what I mean."

"You do not run this school, fledgling. I and the other teachers handle that without student input. Either you attend the classes in the order we prescribe or you find another school."

"This is the only school here!"

"It is, but there are other cities." *And there are schools that will happily take your money and put you in the class you want to be in where you will fail. Don't be an idiot, fledgling.*

He trudged to the baskets where students kept their belongings, collected his things, and left.

Addya shook her head. *You came all the way from the east to study and give up when you can't get your way? Pull yourself together and come back.* She let the practice continue for a few minutes longer before parrying her student's last thrust. "All right, that's enough for–"

The front door opened again then banged closed.

"Sorry," a small voice chirped.

Addya threaded her way through the other students to the little fledgling in a blue tunic. "Hello, Kia. Who are you here for?"

The page came forward and offered a folded paper. "For you."

"Who is 'you?' Specifically name the person and what you have if you know."

"For–for Addya Dace. It's a note. The steward gave it to me."

Addya knelt and took the paper. "Thank you, Kia. You did very well. Return to the steward and report your errand finished."

Kia ran out.

The paper, an invitation to the coronation, was printed in blue ink on white paper. A handwritten note in the corner advised her to come in formal dress if she wanted to avoid being pressured into the tournament. The familiar handwriting needed no signature.

"OOOooo. You get to go to the coronation?" Vri asked.

The fledgling stood up on the tips of his talons to catch a glimpse of the paper over her arm.

Addya tapped his beak with the paper. "You shouldn't read someone else's mail."

"Are you going to be in the tournament?" Vri hopped up and down like a finch. His tan and gray feathers only added to the appearance.

"No." Addya shook her head.

The whole class groaned.

"Artificial fights are no less silly than unnecessary real ones." Addya set the invitation on the table.

"But you'd win for sure!" Caden hung his practice blade on its peg on the wall.

"Do you think so? I might. I might not. Even if I participated, what does that prove?" Addya perched on the edge of the table. "That I can win an artificial battle? That I can lose well? That I can be injured for no reason? No, fledgling. I do important work for the crown. Being injured on the off chance I can prove that I am great? Worse than useless."

"Isn't it like practicing against someone with a skill closer to yours? You only ever get to practice against us fledglings." Vri tipped his head to one side.

"I spar with the other teachers when we can all spare the time."

"How is that different?" Caden asked.

"Emotions run high in tournaments as they do in real fights. Sometimes the only real difference is the edge on the blade. No, my dears. I get enough realistic practice in my missions for the crown." She clicked her beak a few times. "Quickly now. Put your equipment away and gather your things. It's time to go. The next class is coming soon."

Most of the class did as she asked and darted out. Vri and Caden stayed to fluff the feathers over her ear hole about the tournament for a while longer before they, too, left.

Addya chuckled as the last two left, then put the money in the strong box and checked the lesson plans she and the other teachers had decided upon for the next class.

Addya checked her pale gray gown in the polished metal mirror. She would have preferred a shade of blue to honor the new king and queen, but Evryt didn't need her in her official capacity today, so her social status would only allow her to wear the royal colors as ornamentation on a gown rather than the color of the gown itself. The embroidered flowers were in a variety of colors to match the dyed fur collar of the dress. Her dark tail, sticking out of the back slit of the dress, contrasted nicely with the gray material.

After checking the beads in her crest feathers, Addya left her home behind the fencing school and walked along the walkways. Her toe talons clicked on the wooden bridges as she made her way to the grand stairs leading to the castle itself at the highest point of the forest. Most of the castle took advantage of the canopy's shade, but towers stretched upward, disappearing through the trees.

The grand stairs were wide enough for ten armed and armored Aelstrians to walk shoulder to shoulder without touching and extended some fifteen steps up. The actual stairs themselves were not visible through the sea of brilliant gowns and glittery tunics. Addya took her place at the end and advanced slowly as those in front of her waited for the herald to announce them.

By the time her turn came, the sun had gone from on the horizon to fully set. The waiting crowd amounted to only her and a few others.

A young hen in a yellow-edged blue herald's tunic took Addya's calling card and turned toward the gathered assembly. "Royal Courier Addya Dace."

Addya entered as musicians played a lively tune. She searched for a friendly face. Across the way, Countess Yarek stood with her retinue around her and carried on a conversation with Uri, her nephew, if Addya remembered properly. No doubt, Uri would be regaling his aunt with lamentations of how Addya's school failed to recognize his greatness. Let him grouch. All of Addya's teaching staff had long ago agreed that bad publicity was better than dead students.

As she scanned the room, she picked out other pockets of nobility and made a mental note to pay her respects at the proper time. Aside from the major landed nobility, there were a number of lesser ranks and those with purely court titles. Each had their personal guards and aides. Many of the attendants nibbled on fruits, cheeses, or seedy breads from the reception table.

The throne on the dais at one end was a large golden nest with soft blue pillows. If the pillows were exchanged for red, the throne was a perfect mimic of the one in the original capital city, which Countess Yarek occupied and had so humbly renamed Yarekia.

Something tugged on the right side of Addya's gown. She looked down at the fledgling page whose royal tunic clashed garishly with his reddish-brown feathers.

Addya crouched to his level. "Yes, Havi?"

He studied his talons and stammered a few syllables. "Courier Addya Dace, the-the countess said if-if I saw you to tell you somefing."

A little too early from the nest, I think. "Go ahead, Havi."

"Um, um, I ..." He faltered and squinted at his talons.

"Who is the message for? Who is the message from? What is the message?"

"Oh, yeah. Courier Addya Dace, C-countess—um—Countess Tala Yark said if you could go see her."

"Good work, Havi." *Your delivery needs a little*

work, but at your age, perfect.

He peeked up at her. "Really?"

"Really. Now return to your post."

He darted away.

Addya looked across the room at the rotund countess still holding court with her nephew and a few retainers. *Might as well get it over with.* Addya wove her way through the crowd to the countess and stood at the polite distance of a full wingspan to await acknowledgment.

Uri tapped his aunt's shoulder and pointed.

The countess turned her narrow gaze on Addya and looked her up and down. "Well, Courier." She clacked her beak. "You expelled my nephew?"

"No, Countess. He had a misunderstanding about the way the school operates. I corrected his misunderstanding, but he was not willing to continue, so I refunded part of the day's fee, granting him half even though the session had nearly ended. He may return for tomorrow's lesson if he wishes, but the school is run in the manner that the teaching staff decides, not the students."

Yarek reached up and preened Uri's head feathers. "We won't be bothering with that. If you can't recognize his obvious skill, then there are other schools." The countess pivoted, turning her back to Addya.

And they'll be thrilled to take your money.

Addya stepped back and continued making the rounds, greeting both landed and court nobility. She'd finished and gone to the buffet table for some fruit and candied beetles when the heralds all around the room trilled a long, high note. She stepped back and turned her attention to the royal balcony opposite the throne. Evryt and Jianna stood on the edge of the platform two wingspans apart. They leapt, launching off from the edge, extending their wings, and gliding toward the throne. Their blue and silver tunics rustled in the air. The pair landed on the top of the dais next to the nests. Jianna's handmaid trotted out and helped Jianna wrap the skirt of her gown around her slender waist.

The pair stood behind the thrones. Evryt's feathers, a darker shade than Addya's own, were perfectly preened with blue and silver beads in his crest. Jianna's tan feathers were fluffier, almost like an owl's. There were times when Addya wished her own feathers had such delicate texture, but that sort of softness didn't run in her family line. The stiffer, more rigid feathers had their place, too.

The crown prince and his wife clasped hands and spoke in unison. "We swear to uphold the laws of Aelstria, setting aside our personal objectives for the service of the people, to rule them in the best interests of the nation, and to preserve Aelstria for our fledglings." They stepped into the golden nests and settled with their legs folding up neatly beneath them.

All in attendance trilled, filling the air with a lackluster but cheerful noise. Addya added her own trill at the pitch that balanced tone and volume perfectly. With so many present, the sound should have hurt her ears. As she scanned the room, some beaks were open, but there was no movement in the syrinx.

Sore losers. He's king by right of inheritance,

whether you like it or not.

The trill had lasted almost a full minute when the heralds in their blue and yellow tunics dispersed through the crowd encouraging a space in the middle of the throne room. Addya reloaded her plate from the buffet and drifted toward the wall, finding a place to perch where she could watch the coming entertainment.

Let's see. If I know those two, Jianna chose tumblers, and Evryt wanted the tournament.

A trio of brilliantly-colored performers walked to the center of the room. At first, Addya thought they were wearing some kind of sheath on their wing feathers to make them such brilliant, unnatural hues, but she squinted and leaned closer.

No, they're dyed.

Each wing feather was a different color. Even the face and crest feathers were unusual shades.

Addya tilted her head to one side and popped a candied beetle into her beak. *That took some dedication and a very light plumage color to start with.*

The trio knelt and touched their beaks to their chests before launching impossibly high into the air. They reached the same height in their arcs – almost to the ceiling – but descended at different rates by adjusting the extensions of their wings. They landed in a tower with each tumbler on the raised hands of the other. A trill, one less impressive than the one that had celebrated Evryt and Jianna's ascension, rewarded the excellent timing and balance. The routine continued with the acrobats tossing each other and landing in bizarre contortions. Jianna's appreciative trilling rose over everyone's.

While the tumblers continued, Addya made her way behind the crowd and along the wall back to the buffet table where she discarded her plate in the wash pail for the kitchen and picked up a bowl of fruit juice and a hand-sized towel. She watched over the heads of the crowd as the rainbow-colored performers shot up into the air. They joined hands and slowly glided back down.

She carefully lapped up the juice in the bowl, and then dabbed her beak with the towel before discarding both in the wash pail.

The two smaller tumblers, curled into tight balls, spun up into the air, first one then the other, over and over again while Addya made her way back to her previous place. Trilling filled the air. Jianna caught Addya's eye and waved her over.

Up there in front of everyone is the last place I want to be.

Still, she could hardly deny a royal invitation. Kicking her skirt out in front of her to avoid tripping on the hem, she walked up the dais steps.

"Perch here. You'll see better." Jianna patted the floor next to the nest.

Addya settled near Jianna and straightened out her skirt.

Jianna leaned closer. "Aren't they wonderful?"

All three were in the air and pushing off from each other and from the walls to change directions and stay in the air.

"I've never seen anyone like them."

Jianna tipped her head and looked at Addya from the corner of her eye. "I heard the herald announce you. When are you going to use your real title?"

Sometime about a week after I'm dead, perhaps. "'Royal courier' is my real title. Being head of the couriers doesn't change that."

"No, I mean your other title."

Addya tipped her head down and peeked up at the new queen. "The one we agreed not to speak of in public? This is very public, you know."

"No one is listening."

"There are ears everywhere, and your ascension is going to be difficult enough. Don't complicate it."

The tumblers floated downward and landed on their knees with their heads bowed. Addya joined in the appreciative trilling as the trio strutted out through the crowd.

The adulation of the crowd faded before the heralds escorted three males and a female to the center. Each had a practice sword in hand and wore a colored tabard matching one of the main provinces. One wore red and black for Countess Yarek's domain. One wore the gold and green of Count Quetik. The third had Count Azel's orange, and the last sported the duke's gray and white.

Addya tilted her head toward Jianna. "Thank you for the warning."

"I know how much you hate these things." She reached over and preened a feather on Addya's arm. "Just once, though, I wish you'd consider entering one. I think you would show all these down-feather-brained idiots how to use a sword."

"I wouldn't discount them so quickly. I am skilled, but I'm a long way from perfect."

The herald introduced all four fighters then stepped away. The quartet broke into pairs and began their first bouts without first acknowledging the new king and queen. An angry hiss rose from the audience, and Addya joined the show of displeasure. She didn't have to wonder who encouraged such an amazing breech of etiquette with three of the four representing Evryt's political opposition.

Yarek's black-feathered fighter made a quick, easy evasion of his opponent's thrust and drove a riposte into the other's chest. Before the opponent could declare the hit good, Yarek's fighter stepped past and waited for the other pair to finish. He tapped his toe talons on the stone floor. As soon as a perfectly aimed thrust ended the other fight, Yarek's representative launched to the attack before Quetik's fighter could bring his sword up. Another hiss rose from the crowd. When Yarek's fighter won a moment later, the hiss intensified.

The four paired off in a different combination and began again. As before, the black-feathered one finished within a few short moves. He leaned his weight on the practice sword with its point on the floor. The thin metal bowed in a gentle arc under his weight. The other fight ended shortly after, but this time Quetik's representative took the attack to his remaining opponent. The match lasted a little longer this time, but Yarek's fighter came out victorious again.

The bouts continued a few more iterations until each had fought the other at least a few times. Every time, the duke's and Count Azel's combatants lost quickly, and the remaining two battled it out until

Countess Yarek's fighter won.

Jianna leaned closer. "Is he really that good, or are the others that bad?"

"He's good. Don't doubt that. He's quick. He has good form. I'm not sure I would win against that one."

As Jianna leaned away, her eyes narrowed. "You? Without a problem."

"I'm less certain."

The last battle ended. All four of the combatants breathed in deep gasps.

Countess Yarek waddled into the middle of the room. "Is there no one of sufficient challenge for my guard captain?"

Murmurs flitted through the crowd.

Jianna groaned. "Such arrogance."

"What about you, Courier?" the countess' piercing eye turned on Addya.

Addya gestured to her skirts. "I'm afraid we won't know that answer today. My invitation said to come in formal attire, not fighting gear."

"Convenient, isn't it?" Yarek's eyes narrowed before she waddled back to her entourage.

The four fighters formed a line in front of the dais. They started to their knees but only one got all the way down. The others only made it halfway then popped back up and walked out through the crowd. Hissing crescendoed. Count Quetik's fighter, the only hen, knelt, tipped her head down, and fluffed out her head feathers. After a few moments, she stood and left.

The musicians began a stately tune and pairs of dancers filled the floor. Evryt invited his wife to dance. Addya descended with them then stepped away to congratulate the combatants' sponsors, but as she did, she mentally replayed the bouts. All fighters had their weaknesses, and given the sentiments Yarek expressed so openly, Addya had no doubt that she would be crossing swords with that champion at some point.

Evryt stood with his wife and his court officers on the landing platform as airships landed long enough to load their passengers and lift off again. The whole morning so far had been one long line of airships and farewells, all perfectly cordial, but some more sincere than others. Now only Countess Yarek and Count Quetik remained with their respective attendants.

Count Azel's orange airship lifted off.

The countess' air ship slid into place, giving the basket of the orange airship a good nudge with the top of the balloon. Azel's basket teetered, and squawks of protest came from within. Evryt cringed. That kind of recklessness would get someone killed.

"Big chicks," Yarek muttered.

Her airship landed with a crunch of the basket on the scattering of leaves littering the platform. The door flew open and a half-dozen of Yarek's guards trotted out and formed a double line, one on each side of the door.

Groaning loudly, Yarek rose from the bench

where she'd perched and waddled over. "Congratulations on your ascension, I'm sure, but the throne must revert to my family line as your father intended."

Evryt squinted. "And it will, when the time is right and in keeping with the instructions my father gave me." *No, you will not gain the throne from me if I have any power to stop you.*

She snorted and spun away. The lower hem of her red-embroidered black dress swung back and forth like a bell. The countess walked between her two lines of guards and boarded her ship. The rest of her entourage followed, and the six guards entered last. The airship lifted off.

"Be careful with that one." Count Quetik stepped forward. "I don't trust her."

"With good reason," Jianna chirped.

Quetik huffed. "Make it a priority to get her out of the way."

Evryt's guts unsettled. *Yes, because I can simply will it to happen?* "I have to wait for her to do something before I can remove her. Disagreeing with me politically is not enough. I must observe the law or we lose more than just the proper heir on the throne. You know that."

"Perhaps, but Aelstria would be a better, more stable place without her stirring things up all the time."

Toe talons tapped on the wood planks.

Addya slipped forward into Evryt's peripheral vision. "Count Quetik, what if the next heir in the line believes that Evryt will hold the throne quite well without interference and refuses to ascend?"

The Count turned to face her. "Courier, we must all perform our duties, no matter how distasteful we find them."

A green and yellow airship folded in its sails and landed on the platform with a light crunch. The count faced Evryt and bowed his head, ruffling up the feathers on the back of his neck.

"Thank you for your support, Count. I will make restoring the proper line a priority, but I must remain inside the law."

"Of course. Congratulations, sire."

He backed away a few steps before turning. His retinue followed him on board.

Once the airship lifted off, Evryt blew out a deep breath. *I'm glad that's over.* He turned to his officers. "I plan to rest today. We'll resume normal schedules tomorrow. Thank you. You may go."

Each officer bowed to him then left.

When they were alone, except for the ever-present guard, Evryt offered Jianna his hand and escorted her back to the palace.

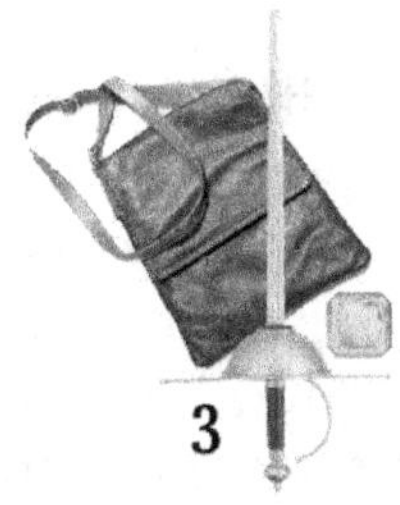

3

By the time the airship set down in the courtyard, night had fallen. Countess Talia Yarek huffed, disembarking without giving her guards a chance to announce her presence. She'd spent the entire trip back planning the details of her next logical move, and if she didn't record her ideas soon, they'd drift away like down feathers in a stiff wind.

She strode across the courtyard to her front doors, which opened as she approached.

"Welcome back." The steward bowed his head as she entered.

Talia snorted. "Send food and drink to my study. Something substantial. It's been a long, aggravating day."

"Immediately."

At the foot of the stairs, Talia paused, studying the upward stairs with a hard gaze. Someday she'd have to have her study and personal chambers moved to the ground floor, but for now, the stairs. She climbed the stairs with a firm hand on the banister for support, pausing midway to catch her breath. At the head of the stairs, she sat on the ornate bench placed there specifically for her comfort and rested until she regained her wind.

Her study, down a long hallway on the second

level, welcomed her with the comforts of a warm fire and wonderfully ornate red and black furnishings. She crossed the intricately woven silk rug covering the floor in the center of the room and perched on the padded divan behind her wooden desk. The ink, quills, and paper in the center drawer of the desk all found their spaces on top, and she jotted her ideas as quickly as the ink and quill allowed, sketching enough detail to recall the specifics later. A general map, a dual list of trustworthy nobility and traitors, and a few talking points for her to use in the meeting she intended to call.

On a new sheet of paper, she began a letter to the duke, inviting him to this meeting to discuss matters of mutual interest. True, the old bird was a terrific windbag, but his support and his army would be invaluable in the coming conflict. Once she was properly restored to the throne she should be sitting on right now, she'd make sure the old windbag didn't get any grand designs of his own.

The next letter went to that useful idiot, Azel. True, the popinjay couldn't find the ground by dropping something five times in six, but his forces were not as inept. The count himself could be easily manipulated.

She scanned through the rest of her list. The lesser nobility weren't necessary. They would do what their masters ordered, and she had ways of taking care of them if they didn't. On the other side of the list, she'd written the twins as traitors. Rach and Orak Anat had no great love for her, that was true, but they were not keen on Evryt staying in charge. Could she get them onto her side long enough to oust Evryt? She had the letter written to Rach by the time the servant door opened. A young, splotchy-brown hen brought in a tray bearing a platter of meat, a bowl of wine, a selection of candied beetles, a bowl of chopped fruit, and a bowl of beans and grains.

The serving hen brought the tray over to the desk and glanced at the papers spread across the surface. "Where shall I put it?"

Keep your beak on your own business if you don't mind. "On the table." Talia pointed to the low table near the fire.

As the servant complied, Talia read the note she'd begun to Rach. Maybe including the twins wasn't such a good idea. How could she properly trust them? She piled all but the finished notes to the upper nobility and slipped them in her desk.

"Send the head of the messengers to me." Talia waddled over to the fireplace table and settled next to it.

"Right away," the hen chirped as she slid out the hidden servant door.

Talia picked up a piece of meat and gnawed off a chunk. With good plans and strong allies, soon Evryt's throne would be as empty as the platter was about to become.

Chal sat in the front room of his little house sipping his tea and grooming the gray-edged feathers on his arm. The trumpet fanfares last night indicated the countess' return to the city, and that meant his brief vacation was over. With that fat, old bird back in town, her study and quarters would be unlocked again, and data collection and analysis would resume. There was no mystery to how the countess would feel about the crown prince's coronation. This might be the perfect opportunity to find enough evidence to get Yarek convicted of treason. Whether Evryt kept the throne or passed it to the proper heir would be a matter of insignificance as long as he dealt with that glutton.

The market bell, mere steps from his front door, rang. Chal opened his drapes far enough to see the entrance. He watched the flood of shoppers entering through the archway. When he spotted a member of his flock, he sat up straighter. She stopped at the edge of the arch and fished around in her pouch before producing a coin, which she dropped. When she knelt to pick it up, Chal quickly drank the rest of his tea and fetched his worn-out tan cloak and a basket from the chifforobe in the foyer. He grabbed a shopping list from the desk and headed out the door.

He recalled the rotation of shops for the second day of the week then counted down the list to the one corresponding to the day of the month. He walked at a leisurely pace to the pottery merchant, making a few unnecessary stops and buying an unnecessary cloak along the way. Someone would need it for a mission at some point, and if not, he'd donate it to a poor person.

Before he reached the potter, he spotted the

member of his flock inspecting a clay jug. She was a splotchy brown hen whose drab coloring and keen mind made her perfect for this line of work. Dehr's current cover was a serving girl in the palace, and kneeling to pick up a dropped the coin indicated she had proof of Yarek's treachery.

He drifted his way toward the potter, making sure to stumble over the cobblestones as he arrived. The shopping list flew out of his hand and landed at the feet of his agent. She leaned over and picked up the paper, palming that one and replacing it with another.

"Oh, be careful!" Dehr said helping him back to his feet. "Crashing into all these pots would be a sad thing indeed."

"Crashing" equals "saw evidence." "Thank you." He took the switched paper and tucked it into his basket.

She held up a pitcher. "What do you think? Should I get this one?"

Chal considered the pitcher but picked up a different one. *"Do I want you to retrieve the papers?" Skies and clouds, no, fledgling. I don't want you to risk being caught in a foolish effort. You're too well-placed.* "This would be better, I think. It has better lines."

She set hers down and took his. "It's beautiful. Are you sure you don't want it?"

Yes, I know you're capable, but I need you in the palace. "I have another that's similar."

Dehr paid the vendor and left with the pitcher in hand. Chal shopped for a bit longer and picked up a small, simple bowl to add to the mismatched collection destined for the poverty-stricken in a couple months. He left the potter and continued on to complete his real errands, fighting the urge to speed up his trip. As much as he wanted to read Dehr's note, drawing attention to himself could be dangerous.

After stops with the baker, a farmer, and a fish monger, Chal returned home with his purchases, took out Dehr's paper, and grabbed the book from his desk containing the current codes. He sifted through the necessary pages and soon had the message decoded.

"I found a map with new borders, a list of nobility on each side of the dispute, and letters about a meeting. Desk. Countess' office." Chal burned the paper in the fireplace then composed his own coded note to the king.

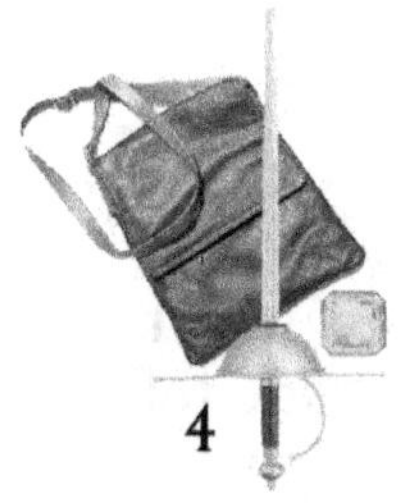

4

Karl left Pferd at the stable and walked through the drizzle to his house, a cottage near the prison tower where he could keep a closer eye on any fugitives he had locked up. The smell of the castle area wasn't quite so intense with the drizzle keeping fumes down, but dismal days made him homesick for the wide skies, sun, and clean air of the old farm where he'd grown up. The property, of course, had gone to his older brother upon the death of their parents, and his sister had married well. As the younger son, Karl had to find his own way, with a little monetary help if needed. He didn't mind. He had a good position that took him out into the countryside often enough to escape the confines of the castle walls.

He entered his little house through the business entrance, which took him into the office in front of his actual dwelling.

A young man stood as Karl entered. "Sheriff?"

Karl crossed the room and shook the man's hand. "Yes, Karl Schildmann, Sheriff of Haufenwache."

"I'm Oskar, and I have a farm northwest of here." He removed his hat and ran his fingers through his short, black hair. "These Aelstrians, sir, something needs to be done with them."

"What's happened?"

Oskar paced away and came back. "Well, sir, this one claiming to be on official business, he comes into our house without even a knock, sir, and he kicks us out of our own house and tells us he's taking over our quarters like it's his right or something. If I could've gotten to my knife, why he'd've never gotten away with it, but he pointed a crossbow at my wife and kid and told us to leave. What could I do, sir? He helped himself to the food on our fire and ransacked the place, looking for our money, I guess, but I got him there, sir. I keep that hid well, and a good thing. It's all we've got."

An official courier acting like a rogue? Something didn't sound right. A quick test would help. "This official Aelstrian, he wore green, didn't he?"

"No sir, red like blood from a new wound. Red with black on the edges, and his feathers were solid black."

Karl frowned. *Countess Yarek's man, but why would he be northwest of here?* "Which way did he go when he left?"

"Back east, sir."

"I'll try to pick up the trail." Karl noted the worn material and patched trousers of the farmer. The Aelstrian thief probably took more than the man could afford to replace. Karl leaned over his desk and wrote a quick voucher for one day's food for a family of three. "Take this to the castle kitchen or to the market in town. That will restore what you've lost."

His eyes brightened. "Thank you, sir."

After ushering the man out, Karl gathered his

supplies for a prolonged journey and left to give his report to his lord.

Two weeks after the coronation, Evryt sat at his desk in the study where Father had spent so much time taking care of the actual business of the country. He no longer felt like a usurper sitting here. All of Father's things had been removed, and Evryt slowly redecorated in his own style.

On the first day he'd occupied this chair, he'd requested an update from each of his officers. They were still filtering in, and today's was the report from the exchequer. As a whole, the kingdom was in a good situation. The taxes weren't too severe and there was a modest balance of funds. Six of the seven provinces were in good shape, too. The seventh was no surprise, and after endless audiences with all the landed nobility over the last few days, he had no doubt why Countess Yarek's was the only province with a budget failure. That assumed her revenue numbers were honest to begin with. Cooking the books to avoid her fair share of taxes would be typical of the kinds of games she liked to play. In any case, a little less on personal decoration and a little more on something substantial would fix most of that problem.

He flipped to the second page of the report. The door flew open and one of Addya's little court messengers fluttered in. The door hit the wall with a bang and the fledgling cringed.

"Sorry."

"Gently, Havi. More careful next time." Evryt waved him forward.

"Yes, sir." The reddish-brown fledgling ran over and stared at his talons. Spiky little pinfeathers on the back of his head needed a good preening.

"What is your message?"

"Oh, uh, uh." He fumbled with a letter in his pouch, dropped the paper, picked it up, then dropped it again and picked it up once more. "A bird flew in with a note for you."

Evryt took the tightly folded paper and pried it open to find a grocery list in tiny print. *That will take some time to decode.* "You may go."

The fledgling raced out the door, slamming it closed behind him. "Sorry!"

Evryt hissed. "Gently!"

Addya had to train these little ones better before they rattled all the doors off their hinges. He pulled the current month's book from his desk. Using the date for a key, he opened to the proper page and decoded the words.

"Suspicious map and other information on countess' desk. Continue to suspect one of my flock might not be loyal. Investigating. Request someone with legitimate business in the castle to retrieve the papers."

He read through the note a few more times and then glanced at the exchequer's report. A message requesting more details about the countess' budget would be in order, and that would give a courier a perfect reason to be there. Did Addya have any in her flock who would be suitable for this sort of mission? Evryt slid open his desk and withdrew Addya's report. She had answered all his questions in great detail, but he hadn't thought to ask if any of her couriers were skilled in spying and retrieving information.

Evryt leaned back and grabbed the pull cord hanging from the wall. He gave it a few sharp tugs and waited. A maid slipped through the door and touched her beak to her chest.

"Send a runner to fetch Royal Courier Addya Dace."

She whistled an acknowledgment and slipped out.

While he waited, he paced the room, occasionally casting a glance at the note from Chal. Evryt had been hoping for Yarek to make a catastrophic mistake, the sort that would justify removing her for good. If she really had made the critical error so early on, then he could settle the whole issue of getting the proper heir on the throne without risking a war with the humans in Schafland.

The door opened, and a herald ushered Addya in. Evryt paused long enough to hand her the translation of Chal's note. She scanned through it as he continued pacing.

She held up the paper. "If this is true, the map and other papers are exactly what you need to remove her."

"Yes, I think a courier could find a way in and get into her study." He pointed to the exchequer's report. "The results of that report get your person into the castle."

"This is tricky. None of my couriers are trained for this sort of work and being caught at it means fighting through many skilled guards between the palace and the gate." Addya rolled the note into a loose cylinder and tapped it against her hand. "I will have to go."

"You, Addya?" He turned and took a few steps toward her. *If something happens to you …*

"Yes, me. Too many of my colleagues have neglected their fencing practice, and I haven't been in place long enough to fix that. No one else among my flock has the same training with a sword, and if it does come to a fight, I'm not sure even I could handle Iado."

"Iado?"

"Countess Yarek's captain. The one who so soundly beat everyone in the tournament."

Evryt thought back to the tournament and hissed. "Him, yes."

"I've been collecting information on him. He's trouble." She clasped his arm. "This wouldn't be the first time I've gone on a courier mission."

"No, no it wouldn't." He covered her hand with his. "You've only gone on a couple every month for the last several years." *But this time, things are different. Surely you see that.* "All right. Finish whatever business you need to, get whatever supplies you'll need, and be careful, please."

"I will. If there's information to bring back, I'll bring it." She bowed her head and fluffed out her feathers before backing away and leaving.

Evryt watched her go and hissed. He returned to his desk and composed a coded note back to Chal.

Karl held onto Pferd's reins and dismounted. The recently harvested fields he'd been traveling through had done a good job of helping him keep up with his quarry's footprints, three forward-facing toes and one backward one, but now at the end of the farmland, the grasses became denser. The ground no longer showed footprints, but he wasn't yet far enough east to get into the brush that might snag his quarry's clothes or reveal direction of travel with broken twigs. So far, the Aelstrian had been keeping a fairly straight course toward the border. There was no reason to assume he'd suddenly change his habit. Karl climbed back into the saddle and urged Pferd into a trot while scanning the terrain for sign of the messenger or a farm house where he might have stopped.

The terrain changed from relatively flat plains to low, rolling hills. As he continued on, his rear wearied of the saddle, and he hopped off to walk for a while. At the crest of a hill, he spotted a wagon drawn by a single horse just leaving a farmhouse.

Might know something of that messenger. Karl swung back up into the saddle and urged Pferd up to a canter.

The driver turned toward him and reined in his horse.

Karl stopped at a reasonable speaking distance, but not so close as to suggest a threat to the man. He wore well-made trousers and a doublet over a white shirt, all of fine material.

"Afternoon, Sheriff." The man stared at the insignia on Karl's doublet before finding his face.

"Good afternoon. I'm tracking an Aelstrian who has threatened a family and stolen from them. Have—"

The man twisted around and pointed toward the farmhouse. "You'll want to talk to them. I just came from patching up ol' Lars back there. He fought one of those buzzards off a few hours ago and got clawed across the arm for it. Not too bad. Bled a lot, though. Scared Hanne with all that blood, but he'll be fine. Not good for her to be getting so excited just now. Good thing they got the harvest in already. He'll have more time to rest if they've got enough firewood, but you best have a chat with Lars and Hanne. They'll tell you more."

"Thank you."

Karl waited until the wagon was under way again and turned toward the farmhouse. He stopped Pferd at the edge of the fenced in part of the yard and looped Pferd's reins around a fence rail. "Hello!"

Rustling from inside rendered the muffled voices unintelligible.

"Who are you?" a man demanded.

"Sheriff Karl Schildmann. I just spoke to the doctor, and I'd like to talk to you about your attacker."

The door swung open and a shirtless man stood there. Bloodied bandages were wrapped around his upper arm. He leaned over and set a small axe down near the door. "Sorry, sir. Didn't mean to be inhospitable."

"That's quite all right. With a wife and child, you have a right to be cautious. May I come in?"

"Please."

He walked around to the gate. Blood stained the cobblestone walkway and the doorframe. He expected a disaster inside, but the couple kept the place clean and well-ordered with simple, homemade furniture and patchwork quilt cushions. A collection of blood-stained cloths was piled in a bucket near the door.

A young lady, obviously ready to deliver any time now, stood near the hearth stirring a pot that smelled of garlic and potatoes.

Karl clenched his jaw. Threatening a family first, and then attacking a man and his pregnant wife? She didn't have any obvious marks on her, and the doctor hadn't mentioned any, which was fortunate for that messenger.

"I've just started supper, Sheriff, but you're welcome to stay." Hanne kept stirring the pot as she gestured to the table.

Refusing hospitality might be rude, but the pot was small and their farm plot was not that large either. With a new mouth to feed, and Lars wounded, they would need what they had.

Karl took a few more steps into the one-room house. "Thank you, but if I'm to catch that scoundrel that attacked you, I need to be on my way soon. What can you tell me about him?"

"Not quite as tall as me." Lars sat on a stool near

the table and gestured to the only chair that had a back. "Black feathers, too black if you know what I mean. Didn't seem natural. Red shirt, no sleeves. Came here about noon, while me and Fritz was chopping up some firewood, and demanded some meat and fruit." Lars turned his gaze to the floor. "We're simple folk, Sheriff. We don't get too much of either one of those too often, sir. Holidays, maybe."

Karl sat in the chair. "I grew up on the frontier. I know what that's like."

Actually, he didn't have much more than empathy for the situation. His family had always kept chickens, goats, and sheep. They didn't eat meat daily, but it wasn't fare for only holidays.

"I told this bird that I couldn't offer him more than some grain and vegetables, but he was welcome to share our lunch. He didn't want to hear any of that. He said he was on official business and made his demands again. Then he came after me." Lars glanced at his bandaged arm. "Got my arm between him and Hanne and took a swing at him with my axe. He's a couple wing feathers short now, but he got me a good one. Then Fritz come out of the barn with his axe, and that bird took off."

"Can you tell me which way?"

"I didn't see. Sorry."

"That way." Hanne pointed eastward. "Almost straight the way the sun rises."

Toward Yarekia, which matches up with the red tunic. "Perfect. Is there anything else you can tell me?"

Lars shook his head and looked back at Hanne. "That's all. Fritz ran to town to send the doctor out, and he planned to get home from there, but that's all I know about the bird."

Karl stood. "Thank you. I'd better be on my way. I want to cover as much ground as I can before nightfall."

Lars saw him to the door. With renewed purpose, Karl strode out the gate to his waiting horse. After unhitching the reins, he swung himself up into the saddle and turned Pferd away from the house. He headed off toward the east, alternating Pferd between canter, trot, and walk with occasional bursts of Karl on foot. He had to catch up to that messenger before someone else got hurt.

Addya roosted on the floor of an airship with her beak tucked under her wing and her eyes closed, but sleep wasn't going to happen. She was tired enough to doze off, but the commands from the fire crew to the pilot and back, combined with the subtle sensation of moving, made sure she wouldn't do much more than drift off for a moment.

A burst of turbulence shook the basket. She hissed, picked up her head, and spread out her wings. Usually turbulence lasted moments, but wild winds continued to buffet the airship.

"Hold on, Courier. Going for a lower altitude," the fire chief hollered from his position aft in the fire box.

The ship began a shallow dive, dropped several

feet at once, then continued the dive. Addya swallowed hard, trying to keep her lunch in place. The air calmed and the ship leveled out. She stood and rolled up a window flap. If they were over the forest, she might have been able to pluck pine needles from the trees, but they were still a long way from trees of any appreciable size. Perhaps by then the winds aloft would settle some.

Squawking and shouting came from somewhere below them. Addya leaned out the window and scanned the edge of a farm below. A small town peeked over the hills in the distance. No sign of disturbance there, so she darted to the other side.

"Trouble below!" the pilot called from his perch on top the basket. "Humans attacking an Aelstrian in Yarekia's colors. Should I set down?"

Addya leaned out the window and spotted the fight. A human woman and a girl with farm implements fended off a black-feathered Aelstrian in the red tunic of Countess Yarek's messengers. A human man lay nearby, unmoving.

"Should I set down?" the pilot asked.

Addya looked up toward the pilot's perch she couldn't see through the basket's ceiling. "No, we don't have permission to land and this is not our official mission. I'll jump out and get to the truth of this."

"How will we get you back aboard? We don't have any ropes aside from the sails."

"You won't." Addya belted on her rapier and slipped her courier pouch over her shoulder as she moved to the door. "As soon as I'm out, return to the capital. I'll travel the rest of the way on foot."

"Understood."

She opened the door and pushed off from the step, spreading her wings as soon as she was clear. The wind caught her, and she wheeled around, balancing the speed of her descent with the need to get to the battle.

She aimed for the fight below and shrieked in Aelstrian, "Back away from them, you idiot, before you cause an international incident."

All eyes turned her way.

As Addya neared the ground, she tipped back, using her wings for brakes. When she landed, she jogged forward a few more steps and ran the rest of the way. The messenger batted the woman's pitchfork aside and stepped toward her. Addya grabbed him by the collar and yanked him back, depositing his tail in the dirt before standing where she could keep both sides in view.

She spoke the human language. "I told you to stand away!"

The messenger scrambled back to his feet and hissed. "I no listen to you."

"You will. These feathers are Royal Courier Addya Dace."

"I on official errand!" He fluffed and took a step toward her.

Addya drew her sword and backed him off with the point of it. "What official errand causes you to injure one and harass two?"

"You not leader of this one." He turned and ran.

Sheathing her sword, she took off after him. He ran to the crest of hill and launched off, gliding into the ravine. She followed suit, but he was smaller and faster, and she lost ground steadily.

She slowed and stopped, breathing hard and fast. "I'll catch you later."

At the crest of a natural rise in the terrain, Karl Schildmann stood up in his saddle. In the distance, a red-clad Aelstrian fled from a blue-clad one, who was losing ground. The blue slowed and turned toward the nearby town. Karl sat and encouraged Pferd into a gallop. While the royal courier hadn't been able to catch up to the thief, Pferd might close the gap.

After a few minutes to catch her breath, Addya walked toward the town she'd seen. She arrived as the sun neared the horizon and walked down the unpaved, rut-marred street. The townspeople watched her with narrowed eyes, and she kept her hands away from her sword hilt.

In the center of the town, she spotted the sign she was seeking: a crossed key and sword. The deputy sheriff would be able to point her in the direction of the surgeon. She hopped up the couple steps and struck the door after the human fashion.

"Come on in!"

Addya slipped inside. The office was simple,

with a table and a bookcase next to a heavy safe. The back wall was lined with two iron-barred prison cells.

She offered her hand to the deputy.

He startled, backing away from her for a moment before offering his own hand. "Good evening. Um, how can I help you?"

"I talk for King Evryt Lixine." Addya patted her brilliant blue courier pouch with the royal seal embroidered on the flap. "An Aelstrian attacked a house near here. I scared the attacker off. Sadly, he injured the sire of the house first. I seek the surgeon."

"Let's go." He grabbed a belt bearing one of the human's black powder pistols and a small pouch then led her down the street as he secured the pouch to his waist.

The house at the far end of the street bore a sign with a drop of blood drawn on it.

"Wait here." The deputy sheriff left her in the street and knocked. He stepped inside and closed the door then re-emerged a short time later with an older human male at his side.

"You'll show us the way?" the older human asked.

"Not entirely. When we are in sight, I will leave. I do not think these feathers are wished for at that house."

The humans made good time for being afoot, but she matched their pace. About halfway there, Addya spotted the human woman from the farmhouse coming toward them. The woman broke into a jog.

"There's Liesel," the deputy said.

Addya stepped in front of the humans, turned to face them, and continued walking backwards until they slowed to a stop. She reached into her pouch for some human money and folded the coin into the surgeon's hand.

"What's this?" The surgeon held the coin toward her.

"Your fee, sir. It was an Aelstrian who caused the injury. I will settle the account when I catch those feathers." Addya bowed her head and fluffed out her feathers then turned east.

"Wait." The deputy reached for her.

"I cannot. I have vital data to give and receive." She jogged away.

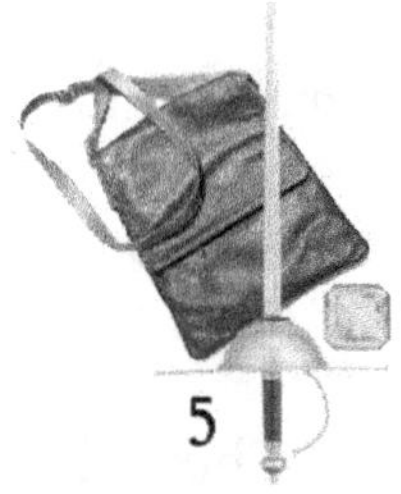

5

Countess Talia Yarek walked into the meeting hall. The huge, U-shaped table took up the bulk of the space. Windows had been thrown wide open to allow in the breezes and the light, so she was pleased that the steward had spared the candles. Finely cut crystals hanging on thin threads created miniature rainbows to bathe the room in color. The effect was meant to symbolize the unity of all the different regions of the kingdom. What silliness. The only region that mattered was the seat of royal power. If not for tradition, and the value other nobility placed on it, she would have replaced all the crystals with red glass. After she assumed her rightful place, she might do exactly that.

For now, she could not afford to alienate her allies. The scraggly-looking Duke Dartin Lixine and the hideously unkempt useful idiot Count Gado Azel, sat at the ends of the U-shaped table, flanking the throne in the center. She strutted forward and roosted on the golden nest with its padding of red pillows. The duke's narrowed eyes were his only outward sign of displeasure.

That's right. Keep it inside your beak. I'm in the proper family line, not you. "I'm glad you both arrived safely. Let's get started."

Dartin gestured with both hands to encompass

the large room. "Where are the others?"

"There are no others." Talia stroked the embroidery on her gown. "We are the only three who apparently have no interest in perpetuating the farce in the bogus capital."

"There are others. The twins for example."

Gado clicked his beak. "Yeah, what about them?"

She fluffed her feathers and shook. "They'll support the usurper for now. They made that clear enough in the capital."

The useful idiot glared at the duke. "That's right. They did. We can't count on them. It'll just be us then!"

Dartin rolled his eyes. "What do you propose, Countess? A frontal assault? Our three armies against the other five?"

"No, of course not. That would be futile, and you know it." Talia shifted in the nest, turning her back on Gado. "We practically border Quetik on two sides as it is. I say we mobilize against him. Defeat him, and then before the others can mobilize, we continue against Countess Jadan, and then immediately proceed south against the capital. By the time the twins catch up, I will be re-installed on the throne as I should be, and they'll back off. Then we continue the conquest against Schafland and drive the humans into the sea."

Dartin jabbed his fat finger at her. "You aren't accounting for either fatigue or losses. Those aren't insignificant forces we'd be going up against."

"You're assuming we're using the same forces the entire time. As we conquer territories, we conscript that region's military and peasantry and keep moving."

"And how will we secure their loyalty, exactly?" Dartin sat back and folded his arms over his chest. "I'm not one for getting stabbed in the back by my own troops."

"Our own tired people quarter with the conscript's families. One messenger bird with a bad report, and the conscript will suddenly be a widower. Our troops get a rest, and we get a fresh, well-rested force for the next stage in the campaign."

The duke preened a few battered wing feathers while he considered the proposal.

"So, what will we get if we win? Dad said to never agree to go to war unless you can get something if you win," Gado said.

"Smart man. You each get more territory out of the deal when it's all over." Talia groaned and grunted as she stood and waddled over to a table in the corner. She snatched up her first effort at a new map and made her way back to Duke Lixine's place at the table. "Come over here, Gado, and see the new map."

He darted over to the table like a fledgling promised sweets.

Talia set the map in front of the duke. "You see? You'll gain the southern two-thirds of Schafland. I'll gain the northern third, Quetik's territory, and the current capital, and Ga–"

The count flipped the map toward him, sending it skittering across the floor. He darted over to get it and then plunked it back on the table. "Where am I?"

"Here." Talia pointed to the northern edge of the

map. "You'll expand into Jadan's territory, doubling your own."

"I get all that? That's good right?" Gado asked.

"That's excellent." Dartin turned the map back around. "And apparently, the twins can keep their own territory, unless they decide to move against us."

Talia nodded once. "In which case, we'll defeat them and split their lands, as well. You may, of course, assign lesser lords to handle smaller pieces of your territory under your control like proper vassals. Can I count on you?"

Gado paced, muttering something about his dad then whistled. "Sure!"

"Rallying troops takes time, especially if we need to avoid alerting the capital. What's our timeline?" the duke asked.

"Let's be ready to move against Quetik in one month's time. We'll stage in the forest here to avoid detection." She tapped the map west of her palace with a delicately painted finger talon.

"Too soon."

"Not if you get your tail feathers moving." She planted her palms on the table and leaned toward the duke. "The time to move is now. Spring has arrived. We need to complete our campaign before winter hits, and this may involve a siege."

Dartin snorted and sat back. "It better not. That allows the others time to mobilize against us and three territories against five is not going to have a favorable outcome."

"No, so let's enjoy our supper, and get you on your way. There is much to be done." Talia grabbed the map and led the way out of the room.

Addya Dace stopped in the trees near the main gate of Yarekia. The flight muscles across her back and chest tensed. The mission would begin in earnest now, and in all the courier runs she had been on, none had involved anything like espionage. If she were caught – but failure wasn't an option. The king depended on her. She fluffed and shook out her feathers.

I'm here on official business as a courier. That's all anyone needs to know.

"Courier."

She turned toward the voice up in the trees, recognizing the tan stripes of her mentor's youngest son. "Gavril? What are you doing here?"

He hopped down and smoothed his feathers. "On foot? No airship headed this way?"

"Do you always meet couriers in the field?" she asked.

He clicked his beak. "I had a feeling you would be sent."

"Who else after a note like that, and that's an even greater reason for you to have stayed in your house." She reached over and ruffled his feathers. "If you're seen with me your cover might be compromised."

Gavril took in the whole area with a sweep of his wings. "No one here but us."

"That you know of. Now pick some flowers or berries or something and head back into town. I'll wait a while before I go in."

His wings fluttered and he hopped from foot to foot. "I want to help you with this one."

Calm down. We're not playing a game. She raised her arms out from her body and fluffed out her feathers. Her eyes narrowed. "No. Too dangerous. You don't think I was sent on this one because it was going to be a simple matter?"

"No, no, of course not, and that's why you might need help." He settled his weight on both feet and pressed his arms back to his sides.

"The whole idea of being the safe house in Yarekia is that no one knows who you are and who your boss really is, fledgling. If you go with me, then you're finished as the safe house here. Is that what you want?"

Gavril hissed. "No."

"Then, as I said, collect some berries or flowers or something so you have an excuse for being out here, and then return to the city. I'll wait a while."

He came closer and pressed his forehead against her tunic. "Just too excited to see you, Addya."

"I know, and I'm glad to see you, too, but we'll have to keep our visiting for when I'm not here on official business." She preened the back of his head. "Go on now. There are some berries in the bushes back that way, and don't look at me on your way back in."

"I will–I mean, no, I won't look." Gavril darted off.

Addya pulled herself up into a tree and perched

where she could watch the gate. *That crazy fledgling! He's going to get himself killed!*

When Gavril approached the gate a few minutes later, he was carrying a pile of berries in the skirt of his red tunic. He kept his eyes on where he was walking, and the guards at the gate let him pass without bother.

Good.

Staying in the tree cover, she hopped down and wove her way back to the shrubs with the berries. This delay Gavril caused would mean she would likely arrive at the countess' palace after dinner, and with that feathered puffball, there was no guarantee any dinner would be left for late travelers. The market would be closed by then, too, so these berries would become dinner for tonight. When she'd had her fill of fruit, she backtracked further and followed a burbling creek well upstream of the city before she stopped for a few beak-fulls of water.

In the distance, a horn signaled the closing of the market in Yarekia. Addya hustled downstream to the road and headed for town. The gates would close for the night after giving shoppers from outlying farms and villages an opportunity to finish their purchases and head for home.

She slowed when she came in sight of gates. A steady stream of Aelstrians was headed out. Many carried bundles or baskets. A few had pouches like hers that hung from left shoulder to right hip.

Quite a few wide eyes turned her way as she approached. The blue of a royal courier brought attention that she did not appreciate. Most gave her a wide berth while they stared. A black-feathered guard stepped into her path.

Color blind or just feeling the extra weight of your own self-importance. "I bear a message from King Evryt Lixine for Countess Talia Yarek."

"You may deliver your message through me." The guard held out his hand.

Addya stepped back and rested her hand on her sword hilt. "Countess? I did not recognize you. You have lost a significant amount of weight, darkened your feathers considerably, and changed your voice."

Former market patrons skittered past, keeping well out of the way.

The guard's eyes narrowed. "Give me the message, Courier."

"It is not customary for a royal message to be given to a subordinate. You see my colors." She tugged on her tunic and tipped her head to the side to show him the blue beads in her crest feathers. "Stand aside."

"The countess does not hold audiences at this hour." The guard fluffed out his feathers.

"Then the message will wait for morning, but I will still deliver it to the countess myself."

One of the other guards caught his arm and pulled him several steps back. He leaned closer and whispered too low for Addya to hear.

He hissed. "Go on through, but your blood is on you if you find a cold reception."

Like the warm and fluffy one you gave me here?

She strutted on through and made her way down a few streets and past the market to the protective wall around Yarek's palace. Why did the countess need to protect herself from within her own city? Did she treat her subjects so poorly that she feared a revolt?

When Addya approached the inner gate, minded by more black-feathered guards, she adjusted her tunic and stated her official business. The unofficial business would hopefully be executed without anyone being wiser.

"It's late, Courier. The countess will not see you at this hour," the leader said.

Addya preened an errant feather on her arm. "Then I will claim my right of lodging." She peered up at the guard without lifting her head. "Or is there reason to wonder why a royal courier gets such a poor reception?"

"No, no, nothing like that. Nothing personal." He spoke with the speed of a falcon in a dive. "The countess does not react well to being disturbed in the evening."

"My business will keep until the morning, but I would like somewhere to sleep, if it's not a bother. Yarekia is a long way from the capital."

"You'll have to sleep in the servant's quarters."

Addya faked a yawn. "That's fine. I wouldn't notice anything more elaborate."

The guard opened the gate and waved Addya through. She walked to the main doors. When the butler, with a more natural plumage of pale tan, answered, Addya repeated the explanation for the third time before being shown down a long corridor to a dead end. The butler pressed on the wall, and a small door slipped open. The servant's corridors within the palace crisscrossed, running anywhere there were walls. Pull chains hanging from the roof marked where the doors were, and small signs scratched into the inside of the wood doors announced what room was on the other side.

The butler led her down a flight of stairs to a basement level and a tiny room barely larger than the bed. He produced a small cylinder of matches from a pocket in his red tunic and lit a lantern. "Here you are, Courier. I apologize that better accommodations are not available."

Addya faked a yawn. "As tired as I am, sir, this will work perfectly. Thank you."

"Dinner has finished for the evening, but I might be able to find you a bite or two if you haven't eaten."

"If it isn't a bother," she said.

"Back in a moment." He bobbed his head once and pulled the door closed as he stepped out.

At least the house butler is friendly.

The hinge made no sound, and the click of the door latch was negligible.

Addya whistled low and set the courier pouch on the floor by the bed.

The room was nothing more than a bed and a wash basin. A simple quilt made of material scraps was folded at the end of the bed. Some straw behind a half-wall would serve for any of nature's calls. The walls and floor were a dull gray brick, and the lantern hanging on the wall cast steady shadows.

A soft knock tapped the door.

Addya tugged the door open.

The butler handed her a plate with a thick slice of bread, a sliver of cheese, a chunk of roasted beef, and a small bowl of water. "I hope this is satisfactory."

More than I expected, certainly. "Thank you. This will do nicely." She took the plate from him.

"My room is at the far end of this hall if you need anything."

"I appreciate your efforts."

He pulled the door closed. The taps of his talons on the stone floor retreated. She turned the lantern down low.

Addya sat on the bed with her tail hanging off the far side and enjoyed her meal as much as she was able. The bread was a touch stale, but the cheese was firm and the meat had been well-cooked. The bowl of water washed it all down wonderfully. She set the plate on the washstand and roosted with her legs tucked under her. She tugged the blanket up to her shoulders and closed her eyes. Sleep didn't come immediately, but while she waited for it, she reviewed the map of the castle, figuring out where she was and planning out the path she would follow to find the information Evryt had sent her for. As she drifted off to sleep, the servants were on their way past her door to their own chambers. Perfect. In a few hours, there would be just a few guards.

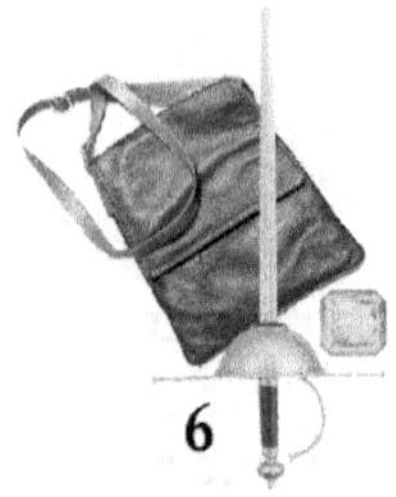

6

When she woke after a few fitful hours, Addya rolled out of the bed and slipped on her courier pouch. She crept out of the room and down the hall to the servant's corridor. Recalling the map, she counted turns and stairs until she came to the door marked "Study."

Addya pulled the chain hanging from the ceiling in the dark corner of the hidden corridor. The servant door into Countess Talia Yarek's study popped open an inch but drifted closed within seconds. After tugging the chain again, she held the door open enough to peek through. Red velvet bedecked with beaded embroidery covered the windows. A squashy divan with an army of satin cushions sat against the wall and served as the chair for a low, delicately carved desk. The stench of heavy perfume mingled with the homely smell of burning wood. Light from the dwindling fire in the fireplace provided enough illumination to avoid tripping and finding the floor with her beak.

A light push on the door opened it with no further noise. Addya crept into the room. The servant door swung closed behind her, making every muscle tense. Her talons clicked on the stone-tiled floor and sounded like snare drum beats in her ear.

Espionage is for the mammals. She winced and

slowed her pace. To be discovered now was to invite execution. The king's reasons for sending a courier to act like a spy instead of a spy to act like a courier made sense, but why had she insisted on being the one?

She clenched her beak. *Too many of the other couriers are all down feather and no talon, and half of them don't know it because my predecessor let them turn into court ornaments. That's why.*

The trek to the desk took half of eternity. Addya settled on the divan and admired the carved woodwork. Where would she even begin? Was it too much to hope that the evidence was in a box marked "Plans for Betraying the King?"

She ground her beak and huffed. The sooner she found the papers, the sooner she could go home.

Addya slid open the drawer in front of her. The scraping sound would undoubtedly be heard all the way in the capital. She hissed. A couple uncut quills, a few corked ink bottles, sealing wax, and a stack of fine paper were the only occupants. She rifled through the papers to confirm they were blank before lifting up on the drawer as she slid it back into place.

The drawer on her right wasn't quite flush with the front of the desk. She tugged on the brass handle and peeked through the opening at a stack of papers. Lines marked on the top one might be a map. Battle plans? The final division of property among the conspirators? A harmless map of Aelstria and neighboring Schafland?

Addya slid the paper out and tilted it toward the dull firelight. It was a recognizable map of the continent all right, but Schafland no longer existed and Yarekia had been expanded. Other borderlines had also been redrawn and showed the influence of the names of other nobility.

The second paper in the pile was a list of nobility and their forces divided into two columns, one marked "Traitors" and the other marked "Loyalists." His Majesty topped the first list.

Addya's eyes widened. *Oh, yes. This is indeed what he wanted.*

The third paper, a simple letter, contained only veiled references to a meeting somewhere, but it bore Countess Yarek's signature and seal. That would be handy for a handwriting comparison in case the lady pleaded innocence. Addya folded the papers into quarters and tucked them into her diplomatic pouch. When she pushed the drawer closed, a cacophonous clang threatened to wake the dead on the other side of the world.

Addya cringed. *Of course, it had to be rigged with an alarm.*

She bolted for the servant door and hoped the door release on this side had a sign on it.

The main door made of carved oak swung open with a loud bang.

"You! Be still and identify yourself!" a deep, masculine voice demanded.

In a single movement, Addya spun and drew her sword. Her crest feathers whipped around, and the beads tapped her beak before they swung back into place. She stood erect and turned her shoulder toward the heavily muscled guard. Like all of the countess's guard staff, he wore a black tabard and had feathers that could only be so thoroughly black through prodigious use of dye.

He came on guard, her mirror image. "Stand down, Courier."

She drew her knife right-handed and straightened her left arm, extending the rapier toward him. "In the name of His Majesty, King Evryt Lixine, clear the way."

Somewhere far overhead, a huge bell tolled.

That can't be good.

His eyes narrowed, and he hissed. The guard tapped her sword aside and charged in.

Addya pivoted on her front toes and brought her right foot around while she retracted her sword arm and used the knife to parry the guard's rapier. Twisting a second time, she reversed position, used her knife to keep his sword at bay, and thrust her sword at his upper chest. The point pressed through the cloth tabard and met the slightest resistance before driving into his body a finger-width below his collarbone.

She yanked the blade loose. The guard staggered back. He dropped his weapon and pressed his hand against the wound. A wheezing noise came from his chest with every labored breath. With the help of a skilled physician, he might survive, but she'd be dead if she didn't get moving.

Tightening her grip on the hilts of her weapons, Addya leapt over the fallen guard and raced down the hall. The corridor ended in the main hallway that ran north and south through the second level of the castle.

The map the king had encouraged her to

memorize flashed into her mind. There were stairs at the north and south ends. The gate out of here was to the north.

Addya turned left. Armor and weapons clanked up the stairs, more trouble than she was prepared for. She jerked to a stop and recalled the map again. The south stairs would drop her near the kitchen, which led to an outside door. If she couldn't get out the gate, she could scale the wall.

She whirled and ran south.

The large, exquisitely carved door to Countess Talia Yarek's personal chambers opened with a terrific groan, and the great lady herself came out. Her Excellency's ample bulk filled out a heavily embroidered, brilliant scarlet gown that would have fit any normal-sized Aelstrian like a tent. Gold beads and glass-beaded chains were clipped to the long, tan feathers of her head crest. Even her otherwise pristine upper beak had been pierced along the edge with what appeared to be diamond studs.

Addya ran past the Countess. Overbearing perfume permeated the air around her. Addya continued toward the rear stairs while the woman hollered and shrieked incomprehensible outrage. Four guards stomped up the stairs and barred the way. Like the one gasping his last breaths in the Countess's study, each guard sported dyed plumage as black as their tabards. As a unit, they drew their swords.

Countess Yarek clicked her jeweled beak. "There's no way out, Courier. Surrender and hand over what you've stolen."

Addya looked back at the Countess and the five

guards coming from the north. "An interesting offer, Your Excellency, but I must decline."

With nine to one odds against her, she'd have to find a way to level the field. On the east side, a narrow corridor led to a window. According to the map, there'd be a servant door down that way, too. If she could situate herself, the guards would only be able to come at her one at a time, two if they wanted to risk foiling each other's blade work. With a little luck, she might even find the servant door. Then she could sneak down the hidden passages to the kitchen and out, if guards didn't box her in.

Addya darted into the eastern hallway.

The Countess's raspy laugh echoed off the stonework. "There's no way out for you there."

She felt around the edge of the red glass window. There was no locking bolt. The catch for the servant door wasn't marked.

Spinning back to the opening, Addya snapped into the erect posture of her favorite rapier style. The walls were only a hand-length to either side of her. There'd be no room for circling motions in here. As the first guard reached the opening of the narrow corridor, she settled instead into the half-crouched form the humans preferred, with her sword hand down near her left hip and the knife at a near right angle to it up at shoulder height. Although not as graceful and precise as Aelstrian Circle, the human style would serve her better in this space.

The guard, a young Aelstrian who hardly appeared old enough to have fledged properly, stepped into the hallway and stood tall, holding his left arm straight out from the shoulder and his right hand back almost to his chest. His shoulders were too square to her and the fencing instructor in her soul wanted to call a hold so she could correct his form. Something in the way he carried himself was familiar about this one.

Wait a minute. I know this fledgling! "Uri?"

"That's right. Part of the official guard." He straightened and looked down his beak. "Iado says I'm actually very good. You were holding me back."

Iado says what your aunt tells him to. Addya blew out a breath. "Back out of this, lad. This fight's not for you. If you come at me, I will defend myself, and this is not a sparring match."

His eyes narrowed. He stepped in, aiming the sword point at her eyeball.

Addya clenched her beak as she swept her knife upward, deflecting his blow over her head. As she lunged, she dropped her aim, turning the kill shot into a dangerous but survivable gut wound.

The fledgling's eyes widened then squeezed closed. He dropped his sword and staggered backward. Another guard grabbed him and hauled him out of the way.

Why didn't you just back off? Addya slid her knife into its sheath and snatched up the discarded sword. The balance was a touch pommel-heavy, but not too bad.

The second guard darkened the entrance to the corridor. Addya resumed her previous stance. The point of the borrowed rapier scraped the wall. No good. She dropped it. The second guard charged at her before the blade hit the floor. Addya jumped back. Her rear foot struck the wall under the window, but his blow fell short. She surged forward, striking his blade to the outside. It hit the wall. She went for the riposte and aimed for the notch just above his sternum. His sword came back toward her neck. She aborted her attack and ducked under his blade, which smacked into the wood paneling on her left. Addya took advantage of his bad blade position and hopped forward. He leapt backward and landed on the hilt of the discarded rapier. When it slid under his weight, he lost his footing and fell.

Addya drew her knife. "Get up."

He grabbed the loose rapier as he bolted to his feet. He held the one in his right hand straight out toward her at shoulder height but kept the left down near his hip.

Mixing and matching styles, are we? Good luck with that.

She stood still and waited for his move, but he held his pose. The mental chess game continued. Then he scooted toward her, bringing his back foot even with his front one then stepping forward half a step.

Addya snorted. *No, I won't let you just sneak into range unchallenged.*

She let him get another step closer before she leapt to the attack. Using her rapier, she pinned both of his blades against the wall and lunged, driving the knife into his gut before drawing sharply downward. Blades clattered to the floor, and he fell to his knees clutching his belly before he fell flat on his beak.

Seven guards remained.

Flint grated on steel. A striker?

Addya hissed, she hadn't counted on a grenade.

Whether it was incendiary, smoke, or poison, staying here would be too hazardous.

She spun toward the wall and felt around for the catch that would release the servant door.

A metal ball the size of her fist rolled into the corridor, coming to a stop next to the fallen guard's corpse. A spark burned from the wick on one end.

Keeping one eye on the wick, Addya pressed on the stones in front of her. They stayed still under her probing talons. The mortar between the rocks showed no cracks or unusual wear. Had the map been wrong?

The wick burned low. Addya turned to the window and punched the rippled, red glass with the bell guard on her rapier. Glass shattered in a cacophony that undoubtedly gave her plan away to the enemy. Gray-green smoke burst from the grenade. She held her breath, slid her rapier into the sheath, and hopped onto the windowsill. Smoke billowed past her. She jumped and extended her arms, locking her elbows. Her chest ached, demanding a new breath of air. A sickly haze stung her eyes.

Once clear of the mist, Addya expelled the stale air in her lungs and inhaled deeply. The back of her throat burned.

Great. Not as clear as I thought I was.

Ahead, four stories of quarried rock surrounding the castle came up at her. The one-hundred-foot city towers in the distance were puny in comparison. Addya turned vertical, using her wings for brakes. At a near stall, she reached the protective wall. Talons on her fingers and toes gripped the rough rock, and she climbed.

Addya coughed and blinked against the tears building in her eyes. She turned her head to her shoulder and rubbed her eye on her tunic. The stiff material gave her no relief.

Voices clamored in the distance. She twisted toward the noise. Torchlight revealed half a dozen figures. Guards, most likely, and there she was with no more defense than a dog in a cage. She could only hope her gray plumage and blue tunic gave her sufficient camouflage in the darkness.

She tipped her head back. *Twenty more feet. Move it, Courier.*

The wall appeared to weave in and out. She blinked hard and shook her head. Her vision straightened out. She coughed again and blinked through the tears in her eyes. Reaching as high as she could, Addya hauled herself up most of a foot.

The burning in her throat eased, only to be replaced by a weird tingling sensation.

What kind of poison is this?

A distant thwack preceded a nearer thud and clatter. Addya glanced back at the silhouettes backlit by guttering torches. A couple were standing with their arms bent at shoulder height. Another was leaning over pulling something up.

So much for camouflage.

She pulled herself up another foot as another clatter came from her right. At least their aim was horrible. If she didn't get over the wall soon, they'd have time to adjust.

Addya stretched for the next handhold at the top of one of the massive stones. She set her talons and pushed with her legs. Her hand slipped. She dug in with her feet and other hand, feeling the strain in her muscles. Another clatter sounded an arm's reach away on her right.

Go, go, go!

She pushed off, caught the edge of the stone, and hauled herself up and found new footholds. Her vision whirled, and her guts threatened to revolt. A couple hard blinks cleared her sight again as she climbed, easing her way left in an effort to avoid ever-nearing crossbow bolts bouncing off the wall.

With one final effort, she pulled herself onto the top of the wall. She and a twin could lie flat, side-by-side on the rough-hewn stone with a little spare room. A thwack came from another direction. Addya dropped flat on the wall. A tug on the back of the tunic warned her of just how close that bolt had come.

When she peeked over the edge, red eye shine beamed back at her.

No, the guards were not lousy shots. They were driving me into this one's range.

Addya drew her knife and hurled it sidelong at the glowing red points. Without waiting for it to land, she rolled off the edge and spread her arms to catch the air and slow her descent.

She landed hard and rolled. When she bolted to her feet, her vision turned white for a moment and everything around her took a quick spin to the left. Addya stretched her arms to the sides for balance and half-ran, half-staggered down the city street.

The cobblestone street tripped her, and she fell forward. A crossbow bolt thudded into the wall of the house beyond her. Addya shoved off from the ground and continued onward. She had to reach Gavril at the safe house before that poison she'd inhaled got the better of her. He would deliver the information to the king if she couldn't.

Her talons clicked on stone as she ran. The alarm bell in the castle tower sounded with clangs that heralded her death.

In the dull light of a half-moon, Addya darted down streets and around corners, bracing herself on walls of the houses and shops as the spurts of dizziness hit her. Footsteps pursued her. She passed through the archway of the marketplace. Tarps covered the fronts of the vendor kiosks.

She stumbled to a stop and leaned on the short wall surrounding most of the market. The fastest way to Gavril's took her straight through the middle of the market. It wouldn't be too hard to trap her in there, but the twirling in her sight wasn't getting any better. The rattle of equipment harnesses and talons tapping on stones grew louder. There might not be time to go around.

"You, Courier," a voice hissed.

Addya spun toward the voice. An Aelstrian man stood in the door of a modest house. The candle in his hand showed a well-worn beak and copper-colored feathers edged with the gray of old age.

He beckoned her closer. "Quickly, fledgling. Sounds like they'll round that corner before you draw another breath."

She looked toward Countess Yarek's castle. Her vision blurred, and this time blinking solved nothing. Whatever that gray-green mist had been, she didn't have much time left.

Can I trust him?

The house swayed in her vision as if she were a newly hatched chick taking her first steps. Other voices and the clatter of equipment came from the far side of the market. Those had to belong to garrison soldiers nearer the city gate who were answering the castle's summons.

Do I really have a choice?

She stumbled toward the elderly fellow. He rushed out to her and slipped under her right wing. He hurried her along, kicking the outside door closed as they crossed the threshold. Inside the foyer, he opened a chifforobe of dark wood and perched her on the floor of it among cloaks ranging from utilitarian leather to beaded and decorated furs.

"No matter what you hear, keep quiet and still." He closed her in.

If I can keep my feet under me.

Addya clenched her eyes and leaned against the corner of the chifforobe. The spinning sensation turned her guts.

Outside, gruff voices spoke words she couldn't hear clearly. Heavy-handed thuds on the outside door startled her. After several seconds of silence, the pounding returned.

"All right, all right. Keep your tunic on." The old fellow's voice had an edge of weariness she hadn't noted before.

The front door creaked.

He yawned loudly. "What is it?"

"We're searching for a fugitive wanted for theft

and murder." The male voice was certainly younger-sounding with its own built-in sneer.

"Murder? Oh my. I was sound asleep until you knocked. I'm sure I know nothing about it."

A heavy weight fell against the chifforobe door.

"Then you wouldn't mind if we had a look around." The younger voice chuckled.

"No, no, go right ahead," the elderly one said.

Addya slid her hand down to her knife sheath. When she didn't find the hilt of her blade there, her eyes snapped open. Everything around her spun, and she pressed her hand against the back of the chifforobe to check her balance.

Where is my – Memory returned, and she blew out a breath. *Used it to distract the crossbowman.*

"What's in there?" the younger voice demanded.

The door on the far end of the cabinet opened. "In here? Just a few cloaks. Want to see?"

Addya tensed. Surely the old man hadn't hidden her in here to turn her over to the guards. If that'd been his plan, why hadn't he revealed her right off?

The cloaks hanging at the far end rattled back and forth. The door closed. Addya gripped the hilt of her rapier and tensed, waiting for the nearer door to open. Her muscles quivered, and her legs were almost as sturdy as earthworms trying to stand erect.

"Fine. You let us know if you learn anything. The fugitive is dressed like a royal courier. The countess will be very grateful for information."

"Absolutely, sir. My loyalty is beyond question." The old one yawned.

The outside door creaked closed and latched

with a loud click.

"My loyalty to the king is beyond question. To the countess?" The elderly man hissed. He tapped on the chifforobe door. "Give them some time to be gone from this area, Courier. Then we'll tend your injuries."

Addya nodded but said nothing. She kept her eyes closed and focused on staying upright.

Light taps of talons on the wooden floor grew louder and softer, with an occasional pause.

"Go on. Go on already," he muttered.

Her legs shook. There wasn't space to lie down in here, or she'd try it.

"Finally." The taps of his talons rushed closer.

The door opened with a groan. Addya collapsed into the old man's arms

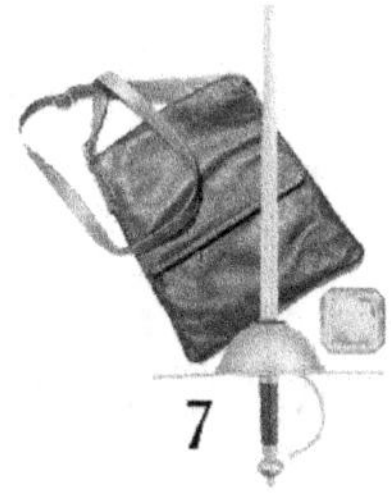

7

Countess Talia Yarek sat at her desk and sorted through her papers. The royal courier had gotten away with the redrawn map, the unfinished letter to Count Anak about the meeting of her major supporters, and the list of those loyal to her and those traitors who actually believed anyone owed allegiance to that young upstart claiming to be king.

Someone had to have told the king about the plans to unseat him. Why else would he have sent that sword teacher as a spy? When the guards brought the spy back, Talia would learn of her betrayer and then ensure both the snitch and the spy disappeared forever.

Talia slapped the top of her desk. She slipped the bell on the slide for the drawer, a futile chore now that the critical information was gone.

The door of her study opened. A guard came in and prostrated himself.

Talia inspected the delicate swirls of color on her finger talons. "Where is that courier?"

The guard kept his beak on the rug. "She escaped the city somehow."

Her eyes narrowed. "How did that happen?"

"We think she got around us and the garrison guards and climbed the outer wall."

Talia rose and hissed. "Useless burdens, the lot

of you. I need the information she took. She cannot be allowed to get that information to Evryt in the capital!"

The guard spared a glance up. "We're conducting a house-by-house search starting where she was last seen."

Tapping her talons on the desk, Talia considered all her options. Either the courier was hiding, or she really had escaped. A vigorous search ought to turn her up if she was still in the area. None of Talia's subjects would be stupid enough to cross her. She'd always made a demonstration of any who defied her wishes.

If the courier had gotten loose, she'd be headed for the king for certain, and the fastest route was through Schafland. If Talia could get ahead of the spy and enlist Schafland's aid, no information would ever reach the capital.

She nodded once. "Prepare my airship. We leave at dawn, and get our troops moving to the rendezvous site."

The guard bolted from the room. Talia returned to her desk and pulled out her ink, quill, and the smaller papers for the messenger birds. How far would Royal Courier Addya Dace get with every province seeking her as a traitor to the crown?

Sheriff Karl Schildmann opened the shed door but stayed out of the path of fire. He tightened his grip on the pistol as his heart beat like a marching drum. After chasing this rogue courier halfway across the country, trapping him in this shed made for an unsafe situation. "Disarm and come out slowly, and you will not be harmed."

"These feathers good work," the Aelstrian protested.

"Then you should have followed the laws of the land. Threatening people into leaving their own homes, injuring people, and ransacking their homes is not lawful."

"It cold! I need good nest, and these creatures not agree."

"Lodging is available for any of the Aelstrian king's couriers at Watcher Reiker's castle." He took a step away from the wall. *Which you would know if you really were official.*

The Aelstrian hissed. "The king. That fledgling's father take throne of others, and took land of Schaflanders. I talk for greater one. Force the false king off throne."

Karl's gun hand drifted lower. More than twenty years had passed since his family had lost half their land in a treaty, but as much as he had grieved as a child, he couldn't exactly say the land had been stolen. Karl's jaw had dropped upon seeing the palm-sized sapphire the Aelstrian king had given in exchange for the land. He might not have liked it, but Papa had accepted payment for the land well in excess of anything it might have been worth. Still, if the current king was on the throne improperly, hindering this courier would slow the rightful ruler's return.

"Let feathers go." The Aelstrian pleaded as if for his life. "I finish errand."

Karl shook his head. "You stole from people and harmed our citizens to commandeer their home. What happens to you is up to Watcher Reiker, not me. Come with me, and you can try to convince him of your innocence."

Metal hissed on leather.

"Disarm and come out slowly. If your cause is worthy, this will require little of your time." Karl brought his pistol back up.

The sound of talons clicking on the wooden floor drew nearer. A black-feathered Aelstrian with a drawn sword darted out of the door and spun away from Karl. Karl struck the sword arm of the Aelstrian then kicked the courier's legs out from under him, knocking him beak-first in the dirt. After pinning the would-be courier with a knee in the small of his back, Karl took a cord from the pouch at his hip and bound the Aelstrian's hands.

"Ow! You say no injury!" The bird squeaked.

"If you came out unarmed and slowly. You came out to attack. Too bad for you that you turned the wrong way. Or maybe not too bad. If you'd actually attacked me, I would have shot you. I'd have to try to miss at this range." He pulled the Aelstrian up to his feet and pulled him over to Pferd, Karl's chestnut gelding. *I was right not to trust you. Haven't met an honest one yet.*

After running a rope from Pferd's saddle to the Aelstrian's tied hands, Karl collected weapons and swung up into the saddle. He kept Pferd on a slow pace toward the home.

Addya lay on her belly, with her head on a soft pillow. The surface beneath her was comfortably firm. A warm blanket covered her from the bottom of her tail to the base of her neck. She stayed still, debating whether to rise or slip back to sleep.

"A courier? After the information we sent the king, he sent a courier?" a female voice asked in a strained whisper.

"It is not for us to second guess His Majesty's choices on such matters," the old man answered. "Sending a known courier was prudent, I say. A potential spy would have been watched more closely."

The female scoffed. "But a courier, really? Most of them can't figure out how to handle themselves if it's not a gala ball or some manner of stately function. They have it so soft, Chal, all of them."

Soft? Addya gripped the blanket tightly in her fists. *Let me get my rapier, and I'll show you "soft."*

"This one's—" His voice dropped to a whisper. "This one's different. There was blood on her blade, her knife's missing, there's the hole in her tunic that I guess came from a crossbow's bolt, and more than a little dust discoloring her tunic, both the gray-green sedation powder and that off-white limestone used in the castle wall. Clearly not the average good-for-nothing court decoration."

"Did she at least get the papers?"

"Yes. In there."

"Good, because after drawing all that attention, there's no chance of anyone else getting near that study." The female let out a long hiss. "I hope you're right about her. She's got a long trip across the continent."

I appreciate your vote of confidence.

"She'll make it. Thank you for the tunic, Tari. I'll get her on the way."

The outer door opened and closed.

Soft taps came nearer.

Addya groaned and opened her eyes to the dull light coming in through a window draped with heavy brown brocade. The furnishings of the little room consisted of the small bed she slept on, a chifforobe twice the size of the one that had hidden her in the foyer, and a dressing table. A large crate in the corner had an odd brown and green canvas tarp hanging out of it along with a few loops of fine rope. An airship's firebox sat under the crate.

"Awake, are we?" The old Aelstrian man who'd helped her leaned against the doorframe.

She couldn't discern color in the dim light, but he showed the wear of age in his well-weathered beak and clothing a couple decades behind the times.

He tossed a dark tunic on the end of the bed. "Good. I worried that you'd taken in something far worse than a sedative." The old man grabbed the stool from the dressing table and perched beside her. "Don't take Tari's cynicism personally. She had a bad experience with a courier who left her for dead to save his own skin."

She pushed off with her arm and shifted around to sit with her tail off the far side of the bed.

"I trust you know where you are and what's happened?" He leaned closer.

She tried to speak but only managed a rough whisper. Addya turned her head aside and cleared her throat. "Yes, I remember everything, but I'm a little unclear on the time."

"Mid-afternoon the following day." He scratched under his head crest. "Your work is becoming legendary. The word is all over town how you killed four of Countess Yarek's guards, stole something valuable, and evaded capture.

"Only one guard was killed. I merely wounded the other two. Not sure who the fourth one is." Addya preened her arm feathers.

"The countess undoubtedly ordered her personal body guard to execute the two wounded and the one tasked with shooting you as you came over the wall. Attributing the death of four to you ensures the tenacity of the remaining guards, who remain unfortunately ignorant of the true nature of their comrades' deaths."

Addya blew out a deep breath. "Getting out is going to be more problematic than I expected. The guards know my face, not just my royal courier's tunic."

She picked up the tunic from the end of the bed. The heavy, well-tanned leather would serve as both clothing and armor.

"I have a cloak that will hide your face. Fortunately, you haven't gone for the dyes so common in the court, so you can still pass for a common worker easily enough." Chal rose and pushed the stool to the low table in the corner. "Get dressed, and we'll get you to your contact. I assume he has your provisions and travel plans in hand."

He closed the door on the way out.

No, actually, he doesn't, but probably better to give him a copy of the information in case I don't escape. Addya stood. Muscles in her shoulders and legs complained about her previous night's activities. *What did you expect? Fencing instructors don't routinely scale twenty feet of rock wall.*

She winced through stretching out the stiff muscles. After unbuttoning the side seams of her courier's tunic, she lifted it off over her head and settled the borrowed one in place. The buttons on this one were stiff and took considerable grouching to get them fastened.

Once properly dressed, she left the room and joined Chal, who stood there with her rapier, a tan canvas cloak, and her diplomatic pouch. The pouch was turned inside out, revealing the black lining and hiding the royal crest on the flap.

"Hmm. That tunic's a bit large, and that shade of brown clashes terribly with your feathers." Chal clicked his beak and handed her the rapier.

She belted on her blade. "It'll serve. I'll worry about fashion again when I get the information to His Majesty."

"You are a different sort of courier, certainly." He chuckled.

She slipped the pouch's strap over her shoulder, and then took the heavy cloak and flicked it around her shoulders. It hung to her knees. She pulled the hood up over her head.

"Walk a little hunched over and shuffle a bit."

Chal picked up a red cloak with black embroidery from the back of a chair and shrugged it on. "The guards are searching for a spry, young woman, not a frail, old prune. Head in the direction of your contact's house but throw in a few unnecessary turns to get there."

He threw the door open and stepped out. Addya rounded her shoulders and let her toe talons scrape across the cobblestones just enough to make a tiny bit of noise.

Her agitated nerves urged her to clutch the cloak around her and run full tilt to Gavril's house, but the attention that would draw could get them all killed. She headed across the street to the wood and stone arch that served as the entrance to the market. A paper tacked to one of the wooden supports showed a reasonable sketch of her face and described her clothes and feathers. The sign claimed she had murdered guards in cold blood and offered a reward of greater than the yearly income of most families for information leading to her arrest and execution.

Addya ground her beak and muttered, "Nice to know the trial would be fair."

"You'd be lucky to reach the courthouse." Chal snorted.

The convoluted path through the market took forever. Chal had them stop at a few vendor stands to shop for a minute or two before continuing on. At one stand, he bought a bag of nuts. At another, he picked up some dried fruit. She almost chided him for the useless errand-running, but she saw his game and held her tongue.

By the time they reached the far gate, Addya's back was stiff from staying hunched over for so long.

As they left the market, a pair of guards in their black tunics and dyed feathers walked toward them. Her muscles were lead-weighted.

Chal wrapped an arm around her shoulder and whispered, "Keep going. We've done nothing wrong. We belong here. We're headed for home after finishing our shopping." Then he spoke louder. "Come along, Mother. We'll be home soon, then you can rest."

Yielding to his guiding arm, she shuffled onward. She forced her breathing to remain slow and even and kept her hand away from the hilt of her rapier.

One of the guards nudged the other in the ribs. "Look at this." He leaned closer. "Get a move on, Grandma! It'll be winter soon!"

The two laughed and continued on their way.

Addya hissed. "True servants of their master."

"They'll get what they have coming to them. Someday." Chal patted her shoulder. "Go on."

A couple blocks further, she turned right. The door of Gavril's quaint home stood open. Loud crashes and thuds came from inside. Gavril stumbled out of his house and landed beak-first on the cobblestones. His torn brown tunic hung on by a few threads, and clumps of tan-striped feathers were missing. He struggled to push himself up with trembling arms.

Two guards stalked out of his house. One hauled him to his feet while the other slammed a fist into his belly.

Just the two of them. Addya's eyes narrowed.

She grabbed the hilt of her rapier.

Addya took one step toward the beasts who needed a lesson in civility when a hard whack on her ankle sent her sprawling in the street. The impact jarred her lower beak hard against the upper one. A firm hand pressing on her shoulder kept her from popping back up.

"Careful, there, Mother." Chal lifted her back to her feet and kept a firm hold. He whispered, "Are you out of your mind?"

She tried to shrug free. "Let me go, Chal. He's my contact. I can help him."

Addya reached for Gavril from too far away. Chal shoved her arm down. Gavril and the two guards paid no attention to what they must have assumed to be a fellow squabbling with his ancient crone of a mother.

He ushered her off the side street and toward the main gate. "Against those two, yes. Against the entire garrison one block away? Hardly. That's what you'll be facing if one of the pair sounds the alarm. Then who would get your information to the king? Certainly not me. I'm too old for gallivanting across two countries."

"Gavril is my friend! They'll kill him!" She wrenched free of his hold only to get caught again a moment later.

"They won't kill him until they've wrung from him every piece of information he has, and that gives my flock time to organize a rescue." Chal pushed her further down the street.

Addya hissed. "Yes, and give that friend of yours another bolt in her quiver to fire against couriers who leave injured people for dead."

"You have no choice, Addya. Even your contact would agree that getting the information to the king is more important than the life of any one of us. We all have our duty to perform."

She clicked her beak hard. "Once you wake up on the wrong side of the clouds, what use is duty?"

Chal's eyes narrowed. "Better that you should get yourself killed and hand the information back over to the traitors? And for what? So someone can say at your memorial service that you failed in your task after attempting a suicidal rescue? Be reasonable, fledgling. Containing a fire in a paper bag would be easier than trying to free your contact just now. My odds are somewhat better if we get you on the way." He stepped in front of her and gripped both shoulders. "So, which is it? Get all of us killed in a fruitless exercise, or let me plan an effective rescue?"

She studied the uneven stones. "If they tracked me to Gavril, what's to say someone won't report you for taking me in last night? What if the next door they kick in is yours?"

"The houses with a view of my front door are either empty or filled with trusted members of my flock. I've done this sort of thing for years. Trust me. I'll free your friend."

"You'd better." She nodded and resumed her hunched posture and dragging gait. "I do not like leaving important matters in other hands."

"I've noticed."

Ahead, the white and tan stone of the city walls blocked all view of the trees beyond except through the same gate she'd argued her way past yesterday. A crowd of Aelstrians and a handful of humans congregated around the gate, trudging forward hairbreadths at a time.

Addya pulled Chal to a stop. "They're checking everyone. Maybe I'd better try over the wall instead."

"No. The walls are patrolled, and gray feathers and a dark brown tunic against white and tan stone would be a trifle obvious, don't you think?" He pushed her into a lower stoop. "We belong here. We've done nothing wrong. I'm simply taking my mother out to the river to enjoy the view and a snack of nuts and fruit. Keep your beak closed and let me do all the talking. All that gray plumage will help you pass for an old woman, but your voice is clearly too young. I haven't got time to coach you."

They joined the crowd shuffling toward the gate. Belts and backsides were all Addya could see from her hunched over position. Her back muscles wearied and trembled. Around her, people murmured about the inconvenience and discomfort of being so tightly packed.

Addya snorted. *Want to trade?*

The guards standing under the arch of the gate tugged off hoods and rifled through bags. She paused. She and Chal would be joining Gavril in that dungeon soon.

"Come along, Mother. We're almost there." Chal leaned closer and whispered, "People see what they expect to see. Act old and frail, and they'll see old and frail."

"How many old ladies do you know who carry rapiers?" she asked.

"Ones who were in the last war, and you would have to be my age to have been there. Trust me, fledgling."

She opened her beak to respond then closed it again. He wouldn't have made it to his age as an agent of the king without knowing a few things.

Noise of a scuffle came from the guard stationed furthest from them. The press of the crowd rolled backward like a wave. The fellow in front of her backpedaled, knocking Addya off-balance. She stepped back onto the hem of the cloak. It pulled at her throat. Chal caught her and hauled her back against him.

She tried to get her feet under her but caught her toe talons in the bottom edge of the cloak.

"Wait, Chal." She stumbled along as he pulled her to the edge of the crowd and then forward.

He stopped and held onto her. "Get your feet under you. Quickly. We have a brief chance to get out unseen."

Drawing her ankle up to her chest, Addya unhooked the edge of her cloak from her talons. "All right."

"Stay close."

She caught hold of his wrist and rose out of her old lady posture. They skirted the edge of the crowd to the gate. The clash of blades rang out from the far side of the wide opening. The backpedaling crowd reversed directions, flowing like a river around a boulder. Aelstrians and humans exited the city through the near side of the gate while the guards dealt with whoever didn't appreciate being searched.

People bumped into her. Some stepped on her toes. Twice, her hold on Chal slipped, but she pushed her way forward and re-established a good grip. Her shoulder clipped the heavy, wooden frame of the gate on the way through, but then the mass of people dispersed in every available direction, many of them running.

Addya jogged to Chal's side and kept his pace, not slowing until there were stocky shrubs between them and the city. He staggered to a stop and rested his hands on his knees, panting heavily.

She led him to a hip high stone and steadied him. "I think we're safe here."

He nodded. "Did not count on an afternoon jog." He leaned back against the rock, closed his eyes, and blew out a deep breath. "Couldn't let that opportunity slip by."

"The timing was definitely with us."

Chal took a couple deep breaths and blew them out. He reached into his pouch and withdrew the afternoon's market purchases. "This will have to do for your provisions, I'm afraid. How's your aim?"

She tucked the bags into her own pouch. "Not my strongest skill, but not too bad."

He reached behind his back, and a belt buckle clinked. "Here." He handed her a crossbow hardly longer than her hand. "These were popular in my day. Not much for power, but effective if you land the bolt in the right place. Bolts are stored in a compartment in the stock. Only a half-dozen, but use them well and replenish the supply when you reach towns that have a bowyer."

She clipped it to her belt. "Thank you. Are you sure you won't come with me?"

"I'd only slow you down." Chal snorted and shook his head. "Besides, I'm the planner in my flock. Without me to arrange the rescue, the rest would get themselves in some dire straits. Go on. I'll see to your friend. Count on it. Only get that information to His Majesty with all haste. Good luck, Courier." He clapped her shoulder then walked back toward the city gate.

Addya watched him through the brush. Once he was gone, she took a bearing off the afternoon sun and turned westward for the Aelstria-Schafland border.

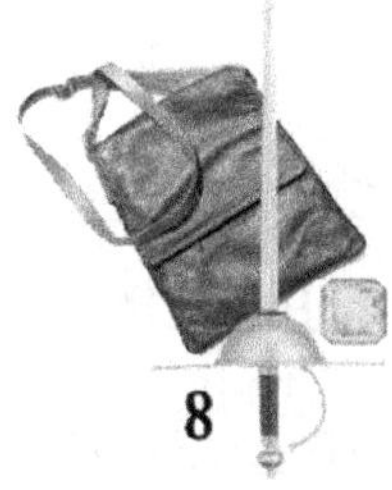

8

Karl Schildmann knocked on the heavy, walnut door of Watcher Hans Reiker's office.

"Come in," Reiker called.

Karl slipped into the room and closed the door behind him. The high-ceilinged room was nearly six yards on a side. The window shutters on two sides of the room were opened wide. The polished wood floor shined in the daylight streaming in. Four sturdy but simple chairs surrounded an equally utilitarian table. The left-hand wall was one huge array of shelves with neatly stacked books and a variety of gifts acquired over a lifetime of shepherding Haufenwache Fold, the northernmost province of Schafland.

The man himself sat at a cherry wood desk engrossed in some sort of written work. His graying black hair had a bald spot like a cleric's tonsure.

The loud-soft clacks from Karl's boots on the wooden floor echoed in the room. He stopped a few yards from the desk and waited for the elderly watcher's acknowledgment.

Watcher Reiker reached the end of the page and moved the paper aside into one of the piles on his desk before he looked up.

A wide smile crossed his face. "Ah, Karl. You've returned, and much sooner than I expected. Were you successful?"

Karl nodded once. "Yes, sir. The cause of the trouble is in prison."

"Excellent work, lad." Reiker gestured for Karl to sit at the table and headed that way himself.

"He calls himself a courier on official business, but instead of a royal courier's blue, this one wore red. He claimed to be a representative of the true monarch of Aelstria on an errand that had to do with removing the current king." Karl waited for his lord to be seated before settling in one of the chairs. "He claims the current king's father was a usurper."

"No, I don't believe that." Reiker sat up straighter. "Well, let me amend that. I believe he could be on an official errand for one of the discontented nobility. The previous king was appointed to prevent war, so although not exactly of the correct lineage, the current king is no usurper."

Karl squelched a frown. "That previous, appointed king was the same one who took our western borderlands."

"Now, Karl, that was part of the treaty, but this current fellow is not his father. It's in our best interests that he remains in power. There are only two others with a possible claim. One is Countess Yarek. There's another rumored cousin with a direct line claim closer than the current king, but I've never met that one. That I know of, at least."

"Countess Yarek has a claim?" He pictured the portly female's last official visit and heard her screechy voice issuing orders and chastising any servant too slow in her opinion.

Reiker nodded. "Three generations ago, the

eldest and rightful inheritor, Yarek's maternal ancestor, would have continued the war against us. The king didn't want that and appointed the younger lad, who of course has now passed the throne to his son."

Karl considered that information in light of the rumors from the borderlands. "That explains why there's unrest in the eastern provinces. They want the countess in place. The west prefers the current arrangement."

"Yes, exactly. You've met the countess. Why anyone would prefer her I can't imagine." The watcher shook his head. "A pity, really. When I met the king and his bride at their wedding, he came across as a good, conscientious fellow."

"Our garrisons are as prepared as they can be in case fighting er–"

The door flew open and a page raced in.

The boy, scarcely old enough to qualify for the post, skidded to a stop in his soft shoes, and pointed to the southeast. "Aelstrian airship coming in." He panted and swallowed hard. "Heraldry shows Countess Yarek."

Karl stood as Watcher Reiker pushed himself to his feet.

"When you speak of evil, it often appears." Reiker took a few steps toward the boy. "Do we know for certain Yarek is coming here, or is she just passing over?"

The boy took another deep breath and blew it out. "She's descending."

He collected his sword belt from a peg behind his desk. "Let's find out what the old bird wants."

Karl followed Reiker and the page out into the front courtyard where the Aelstrian airship was settling into the only open space large enough for it.

The airship's huge, oblong balloon stretched more than forty yards from end to end and stood as high as Watcher Reiker's four-story castle. The red and black material of the balloon fit with the colors of Aelstrian Countess Talia Yarek.

The high-walled basket hanging beneath it was wicker painted a brilliant red. A tube running from the aft end of the basket to the balloon overhead glowed with the fire below it that heated the air.

Gravel crunched as the airship touched down. The door swung open. Six solid black Aelstrians darted out of the airship and formed a line down the length of basket. As a unit, they drew silver swords.

Karl stepped past his lord and drew his own weapon. Around him, the guards did likewise.

Chal paced through the tiny clearing. Dehr and Tari were already there. They lacked only Hensa. Where was he? His cover wouldn't need any elaborate stories to leave the city.

Tari reached for him and missed. "Relax, Chal, he'll be here."

"He should have been here by now." He hissed and paused his restless motion long enough to try for a glimpse of the city through the trees. "Of all of us, he has the easiest way to get here. Dehr—" He gestured toward her with an abrupt wave of his hand. "–Doesn't have that long before she'll be missed in her–"

Dehr wrapped her pudgy fingers around her beak. Cutting his comment short, Chal strained to hear. The grass rustling might have been passed off as the wind, but the snap of a twig would not be. As Dehr reached into her apron pocket where she kept her knife, Tari's hand dropped to the work knife on her belt, and Chal reached behind his back for the handheld crossbow secured there. He hadn't practiced with this new one much, but his skills should be sufficient. The noises stopped, but everyone stayed ready to jump.

A minute later, Hensa jogged into the clearing and stopped, hands in the air. "Just me, just me."

"Where have you been?" Chal checked him over.

The knuckles of his right hand were bruised and blood spots stained his ragged tunic and equally unkempt tan and gray feathers, but there were no injuries apparent in either his movements or his appearance.

Tari darted closer and inspected Hensa's hand. "Get into a fistfight recently?"

"Well, you know, you all get to live in nice homes." He gestured to Dehr. "A castle, even. I do not." His eyes narrowed, but then he laughed, stepping out of his disgruntled beggar routine. "At least, that you know of. You know how it is. Had to stage a bit of a fight for the local guards." He shook loose from Tari and came closer.

Hensa settled on a large stone. "So, what's this caper about?"

"A safe house operator's cover was blown. He's been arrested, and I promised the contact we'd get him out." Chal turned to his castle operative. "Dehr, have you seen him?"

"No, but there's been talk of him." She preened her arm feathers. "The countess has never been this angry before. The operative hasn't told her anything, not even his real name, and she has ordered him tortured if he won't speak up by morning."

"So, it's tonight, then." Hensa chirped.

"Yes, and fortunately, we'll make this a fairly straightforward run. We haven't time to be creative." Chal stroked his lower beak. "Tari, I need you to get his escape vehicle ready. I left it in the usual place. You'll be flying it."

She nodded. "Then I had better get going. If we're doing this tonight, I need time to set that thing up." After tucking her beak to her chest, she darted away.

Chal watched her go. "Hensa, you'll be our distraction, if needed."

He cracked his knuckles. "I'm always good for a bit of distraction."

"Indeed you are. Dehr, what's for supper tonight?"

"Something we can hide a little sleepiness in, I'm sure."

Hensa chuckled and snorted. "So many of the guards have been a little tired lately. They might appreciate the extra nap this evening."

"And I know just which ones need the nap the most." Dehr ground her beak as she stood.

Chal shooed them both away and gathered

berries before he headed inside. He had some feathers to stain.

Sword at the ready, Karl held up his hand to pause the other guards in Watcher Reiker's employ. Aelstrians were not to be trusted, but instigating an unnecessary fight with the second most powerful Aelstrian would be foolish.

All six Aelstrians tipped their heads back and trilled a long, high-pitched note. Those at each end leapt into the air, spread their wings, and whirled, coming down in front of the others. The two pivoted on one foot, stomping with the other at the eight major and minor compass points while the remaining four continued the trill. Once they completed the turn, the pair tucked their heads, raised their wings, and flipped forward, landing in a crouch. From that position, they sprang into the air and landed facing each other. Their drawn swords clashed above their heads before they stepped back creating a space between them with the points of their swords touching.

What's all this lunacy? Karl glanced back at Reiker.

The older man hid a chuckle under his hand and shook his head. "She brought her own entertainment this time?"

The next Aelstrian at each end was now stomping the compass points while pivoting. After two full revolutions, they flipped forward into a crouch then launched and landed next to the previous two. Their swords clashed overhead.

The remaining two in the line worked their way through the same drill, ending in position nearest the door. All six tipped their heads back and trilled that same high-pitched note.

When they fell silent, Countess Talia Yarek moved into the door of the airship's basket. The avian countess was a little short for her race, but what she lacked in height she more than made up for in girth. The sleeveless, embroidered gown sported glittering beads. Her beak still had its rim of diamond studs, and gold beads and beaded chains hung from her crest. The countess exited, waddling under the sword arch. Each pair of guards she passed retracted their swords in abrupt, well-timed motions and followed her.

Once the last had fallen in behind her, she stopped and took in the courtyard with a broad sweep of her hands. "Swords drawn, Hans? Is this your distorted idea of an honor guard? What a fine way to greet your neigh'or."

The voice, too high and delicate for the lady's bulk, brought a smile to Karl's face.

At Watcher Reiker's hand signal, Karl and the other men in the courtyard sheathed their swords. Karl drifted back behind his superior.

"Neighbor is it?" Reiker crossed his arms over his chest. "I recall that the last time you were here, you boasted that, were you in charge rather than the new king, you would annex all of Schafland and enslave the inhabitants. That doesn't strike me as the words of a neighbor."

"Enslave?" Yarek dismissed him with a wave of her hand. "You did not understand. We only wish to aid our technology-de'rived neigh'ors. We would hel' you to reach the current technology. We would shield you fro' the drudgery of a dull, idle life 'y kee'ing your days full with vital 'atters. We would ensure that your children grow in loving, well-enlightened, Aelstrian nests. We only want what is 'est for you under-develo'ed creatures."

Karl leaned closer to his lord and whispered, "Such humility."

Reiker smiled. "Nevertheless, we must decline such graciousness, as we much prefer stumbling our way through our own pathetic existence without your interference. So, to what do we owe this visit, Countess?"

"A request for assistance." Yarek fidgeted with a fine, jeweled chain hanging from her crest, avoiding eye contact.

"From those you perceive as inferior?" Reiker arched his left eyebrow. "Now I am curious. Leave your troupe out here and come in where we can talk in comfort." He turned and whispered, "Come along, Karl. I don't know what's on her mind, but I don't think it's a friendly chat."

The countess strutted past them. For a moment, Karl was sure she'd find the door too narrow for her width, but she made it through safely without even brushing the ornate decoration of her gown.

Karl followed the watcher inside and back down the corridor to his study.

When Countess Yarek planted herself sideways

in one of the chairs by the table, the wood made an ominous creak in protest. Reiker sat across from the countess, and Karl stood at his lord's shoulder.

Yarek preened her tan arm feathers with her finger talons. Swirls of color decorated each one.

Watcher Reiker leaned back in his chair and crossed his legs. "You brought the agenda, Countess."

"Yes, I did." Yarek smoothed the feathers out and then caressed her beaded chains and crest feathers. "A vile creature ransacked 'y study and stole things I need. I think she'll head across Haufenwache to reach her friends. Give 'e your servants to search for her."

Reiker shook his head. "Absolutely not."

"This is vital!" Countess Yarek's eyes narrowed.

"Undoubtedly, but given the threats you leveled the last time you were here, not to mention the actions of a recent messenger claiming to be from you on an errand, I'll permit none of your armed troops to ransack my countryside under the guise of searching for this thief."

The countess clenched tight fists. "She killed four guards!"

"I'm not saying she didn't. I'm just saying that my sheriff will find her." He glanced up at Karl.

"This one?" She aimed one of her painted finger talons at him. "You think this one can defeat a killer and a thief? She'd shred that one with her 'are talons."

"He is not inexperienced with these matters." Watcher Reiker twisted in his seat. "Karl, what information will you need?"

"A description and her general direction of travel."

Countess Yarek huffed. "If you wish to throw your life away needlessly, you seek an average height hen with gray feathers, darker on the wings. She has a sword and is very skilled. We think she is headed northwest."

Karl made a mental image of the description and filed it away. "What is it she's stolen from you?"

"Things critical to these feathers. Exactly what is no concern of yours. I want that confounded cour– that thief found and taken into custody to face the 'unishment for her actions." She clicked her beak. "Honestly, Hans, if you wish to send this-this 'itiful creature after a killer, I will send two guards along."

Thank you, no. I want to be watching for trouble from only one source, please.

Reiker leaned forward. "You will leave with your entire entourage, Countess. Any additional men my sheriff needs will be picked from my own people. When we have your thief in hand, I will send for you or send her to you, as seems most appropriate at the time."

The countess slapped both hands flat on the table and bolted to her feet, toppling the chair. "When your sheriff dies, do not say you were not warned." She whirled and strutted toward the door.

The watcher stood but stayed in his place. "Countess, we have another matter to consider."

She froze, quivering every feather. "What?"

"A black-feathered, red-clad Aelstrian claiming to belong to you made his way across my lands, stealing from my people and injuring several of them before my sheriff caught up to him. He is under arrest and in my jail even now." He stepped around the table. "If you'll come with me, I'll take you to him. I intended for him to face the justice of my court, but in the interest of diplomacy, I'll consider allowing him to leave with you under the condition that he never return to Haufenwache."

"You have a courier under arrest?" She turned slowly, glowering and quivering her feathers.

"Only because he stole from my people and injured them. If he had taken advantage of the courier's courtesy as per our treaty, I would have left him to his errand unhindered." Reiker propped his hands on his hips and widened his stance. "As it was, when I received word of injuries and thefts by an Aelstrian, what could I do? I'll take you to him."

"You do that."

Karl followed the pair out into the courtyard then darted ahead to open the door into his office and the jail. The Aelstrian courier roosted on the bed with his beak tucked under his wing. He peeked as the door opened then bolted to his feet as soon as the Countess waddled in.

The two of them chirped and twittered in their own language, with the Countess' angry glare and fluffed out feathers causing her subordinate to cower and answer in a barely audible voice.

The Countess hissed and spun away from her courier. "So, just as you say. He violated the treaty. He can enjoy your justice."

Karl backed out of the door as the Countess stomped past him and Reiker. Closing the door from the outside, they watched her board her airship and lift off. The firebox in the aft portion of the ship lit the balloon's bag a brilliant orange a few feet up the tube with flickering shadows. The pilot, perched on a platform between the stomach-shaped balloon and the wicker gondola, steered the rising airship toward Yarekia.

Reiker gestured toward the main keep with a twitch of his head. "I'd like your opinion on that little display."

They returned to the study. With a gesture of his hand, the watcher offered Karl a seat.

"I'm not entirely sure what to make of that." Karl righted the chair and perched on the edge.

"I'm not, either." Reiker scratched his short beard. "One thing's certain, she didn't give us the entire story. This gray-plumed female may have done what she's accused of, and then she may not have, or she may have had cause or a mandate. The countess nearly dubbed her thief with another title, which makes me rather curious. This together with the one you caught earlier–" He blew out a breath. "–I'm afraid we're going to be caught between the factions of a civil war."

"Do you trust the Countess to keep her beak out of the search for this other one?" Karl asked.

The watcher snickered. "Do you?"

"Not hardly."

"Mmhm. Watch yourself out there. Take whatever supplies you need."

As the heater roared in the aft compartment, Countess Talia Yarek paced from one end of the basket to the other. It rocked with each step as the airship gained altitude.

She clenched her fist and growled. "Such aggravating creatures!" She whirled and faced her guard captain. "Iado."

The captain rose from his seat in the back of the basket. "Countess?"

"When we've gained some distance from Hans Reiker's prying eyes, you and your men glide down there and find that courier. I want her back in chains, and I want the documents she stole from me."

"And if the humans reach her first?"

"Kill them. Then perhaps Reiker will listen to me next time."

Chal kept his hand pressed firmly to the inquisitor's arm even as the old bird crumpled to the floor in a pile of bones and old feathers. In the distance, Dehr kept up a conversation with the guards, who were coming a quarter hour too early. She had always been very skilled at making small talk.

While he stripped off the inquisitor's heavy

cloak, he compared his recently dyed feathers with the old inquisitor. The match wasn't quite perfect, but it would work well enough for this evening's excursion. People saw what they expected to see.

Once he'd freed the inquisitor of his cloak, Chal dragged him across the room and stashed him on the far side of the bed. Hands quivering with adrenalin, Chal withdrew a few thin cords from his pouch. The rasp of his scaly hands against the leather of his pouch was loud in the silence.

He froze. Silence? Sure enough, Dehr's conversation had ended. Chal left the old buzzard where he lay. The drug in that thorn would have to keep the inquisitor down for at least the next thirty minutes. Risky, but if those guards entered before Chal was ready, this whole scheme would be for naught.

Talon taps on the stone stopped in front of the bedroom door as Chal swept up the cloak and tossed it around his shoulders. Before it had settled into place, he had the clasp fastened in front. As he pulled the hood up, the doorknob turned. Chal snatched up the inquisitor's toolkit as the door opened.

A guard stepped into the room while the other remained in the hall. "Your services are needed."

Chal kept his head down and recalled the voice training he'd done during the last court party. "Yes, I know." He pushed past the guards. "And I know the way."

"We'll keep you company, anyway." The second guard gestured down the hallway.

Chal hissed and strode toward the stairs.

They passed darkened windows, left the castle

and headed for one of the towers. Once inside, they had to go no further. Addya's safe house contact–she'd called him Gavril, hadn't she–lay in a disheveled mess in the middle of the floor. Patches of his tan feathers were missing, revealing heavy bruises from a beating and blood from the torn out feathers. One bare leg had a scabbed over gash. His wrists were manacled, and the chain ran through a pulley in the ceiling grate overhead to a crank mounted on one wall.

"Leave," Chal ordered as he lit a candle from the toolkit and withdrew some small knives.

"That's not–" one of the guards began.

Brandishing one of the knives, Chal pivoted one slow step at a time. "Do I tell you how to do your job? Fledgling? Leave or the Countess will hear of it!"

Narrow-eyed the two guards backed out of the room and closed the door.

"Can you walk, fledging?" Chal whispered in his own voice and knelt next to the scruffy pile of feathers in the middle of the room.

"Maybe, wif som'elp."

"I'm with you all the way to your exit, and then you'll just have to ride safely." He took a pick from his pouch and inserted it into the lock on the first manacle. "Holler."

"Whuh?"

"Holler, you fool, or we'll be found out. I'm supposed to be the inquisitor sent to get information from you by any means necessary."

"How'd I know you're not?"

The lock popped open on the first manacle, and Chal flipped the edge of the cloak back to show the dyed feathers on his forearm. "You ever seen a color pattern like that? Now holler."

"Still a trick."

Chal shook his head and modulated his voice. *Have to get it right on the first try.* He shrieked like one in sudden pain.

Outside the door, the guards laughed.

The second manacle popped loose, and Chal shrieked again to cover the sound of the chain rattling. He slipped his shoulder under Gavril's arm and stood, bringing a realistic groan from the safe house operator.

"Let's go." Candle in hand, Chal led Gavril to the grate in the floor.

"Where we goin'?"

"Down the drain, fledgling. Don't worry. It's a storm drain, not a sewer drain." Chal set Gavril down and shrieked again to cover lifting the grate away before hopping down a couple feet to the dry floor of the drain. "Hand me the candle and come on."

Gavril slid to the edge of the drain, and Chal helped him down. His back muscles twinged with the effort, but he'd rest later.

The storm drain was tall enough to walk in if they hunched over some. With a firm grip on Gavril's arm, Chal led the way, balancing speed with caution until they'd made the third turn. At that point, the guards would need to be incredibly lucky to randomly pick the right path. Counting off turns as they headed downhill and beyond the wall, Chal had to support more and more of Gavril's weight as the exertion caught up with the wounded fledgling.

Up ahead, another light flickered and bobbed. Chal helped Gavril down by the stone wall of the drain and used the inquisitor's heavy cloak to shroud himself, Gavril, and the candle.

"Chal?"

The whispered voice echoed weirdly in the tunnel but sounded familiar, and Chal recognized his own people anywhere. Tari was not supposed to be here. She wasn't even supposed to know the escape route.

Once the echoes faded, Tari called again, closer. "Chal?"

Chal hissed and threw off the cloak. "What are you doing here?"

"With the shape his leg's in, I thought maybe you'd need help with him. You won't be able to sneak this one out while someone picks a fight nearby."

Wait a minute. Dehr only said he was in bad shape. She didn't give details about the injuries. And how would you how I got the courier out? His heart sank to his toe talons. *Why you? What were you offered? What are you being threatened with?* He squelched his suspicions. There might be a reason, a logical reason, for how she knew too much. *I'll find out. Don't you doubt that, and if you've switched sides, there are ways to deal with that, too.* He grabbed the candle and helped Gavril up. "We could use your help, certainly."

She darted forward and supported Gavril from the other side. With the burden halved, they made better time and got to the exit minutes later. The small airship was there, inflated, and ready for lift-off. They helped Gavril into the basket, just big enough to roost in. Chal climbed up to the pilot's perch.

Tari hesitated then secured the door. "I thought you hated flying."

"I'm not fond of it. That's for certain." Chal snorted and situated himself with the guide ropes. "Change in plans. Messenger bird came right before we started. New destination. No time to explain. Go home, Tari. Thank you for your help." He lifted off and turned toward the Schafland capital.

Once out of visual range, he'd land somewhere, dress Gavril's injuries, and sleep until morning before heading for their original destination. Once Gavril was situated somewhere safe, Chal would come back and get to the bottom of his own mystery. He'd suspected one of his flock, but certainly not Tari. There had to be a reason.

9

Addya swallowed the last of the dried fruit and stuffed the empty bag back into her satchel. She couldn't delay a visit to a town any longer. The two scraggly pieces of dried apple she'd just had for breakfast wouldn't hold until lunch. A detour to town would waste time, though. The fastest, straightest course possible would be best. The timing for the countess's plans could not be more perfect than any day now. Perhaps a farmer would sell her enough food to keep her going for another day or two, provided that other dolt of a messenger hadn't given all Aelstrian couriers a chipped beak with his thieving ways.

From her roost high in a tree, she hopped from branch to branch to the edge of the copse. The last bit of forest at the border between Schafland and Aelstria was the end of her tree cover. Terraced hills with the remnants of their crops dotted the rolling grassland. Herds of cattle grazed inside fenced enclosures.

A shadow passing over the land drew her attention to a green and brown airship in the sky. The basket couldn't hold more than one person, and then only roosting, and perched on top was a rust-colored Aelstrian with gray feather edges. Addya thought back to her escape from Yarekia, and happily ground her lower beak against the inside surface of the upper one. She knew those rusty feathers and the cloth of the airship. If Chal had done his job, then the occupant of the basket could only be Galvin.

Good work, Chal.

Movement on the ground pulled her gaze away from the airship. A lone human on a horse crested one of the nearer hills. The male had blond hair and pale eyes. Patches of dust covered his dark pants and leather doublet. The heraldic symbol on his shoulder marked him as a servant of Haufenwache's Watcher, Hans Reiker.

Addya squinted. *I know this one from somewhere.* Thinking back through her dealings with Reiker, her eyes widened, and she stifled a startled squawk. *He tracks fugitives.*

Normally, she would have welcomed an encounter with one of Watcher Reiker's men. The Schaflander was a good man and employed only honorable men, but she'd caught a glimpse of Countess Yarek's airship yesterday. Without a doubt, the despicable female's tale of Addya's "crimes" had been embellished. Would she be given a chance to set the record straight or had this rider been ordered to shoot on sight? Her hand rested on her courier pouch. She couldn't risk it.

Addya froze in place. Movement would give her away. If she stayed totally still, her tan cloak, gray feathers, and brown tunic might be invisible against the tree trunks on a quick glance.

At the far left edge of her peripheral vision, a shadow moved contrary to the airship above.

Keeping her head still, she turned her eyes to the shadow. A half-dozen of the countess' goons slunk along a slope. Iado, with the crimson beads in his crest, led the way. He prepared a full-sized crossbow. Reiker's man wouldn't spot them until he was on top of them. Unlike her contact's troubles in the city, there was no flock of King's Agents to turn over responsibility to.

Under the cloak, Addya's hand drifted over to the mini-crossbow Chal had given her. She'd never fired it, so her aim would be pathetic. Even if she didn't hit Iado, surely the clack of a crossbow would serve as a good warning to the rider.

She narrowed her eyes. There were only six shots. She'd best save them for when she had no alternatives. For now, a good shout should work just as well.

Addya drew a deep breath and screeched. "Hey, Iado! Your beak is chipped, and your feathers need preening!" *That should do it.*

She darted back further into the trees. A bolt flew past her shoulder and embedded itself in a tree trunk with a thwack. She jumped down, narrowly missing another bolt that passed overhead. The moment her talons hit the leaf litter, she pushed off and ran flat out. Whenever she could, she put a huge tree trunk between her and her pursuers.

A loud pop was followed by a bang.

She clenched her beak tighter. *Human pistol.*

Getting hit by a bolt was no joy, but those black powder pistols threw metal balls hard enough to pierce some metal armor. Her leather doublet wouldn't give her any protection.

The trees around her thinned out, becoming shorter and scrawnier. More light bled through the canopy, going from frail spots on the dirt and understory to largish blobs that crowded out shadows.

She turned toward the deeper parts of the forest. Crossing back into western Aelstria would add time to a trip that needed to be sped up. The hills had served as a hiding place for Iado's men. The terrain would do the same for her.

Addya stopped with her back to the last of the large trees and peeked around the edge. Five midnight-black guards were moving forward in a line, carefully checking around tree trunks and in canopies.

Where's the other? Did the human get him, or is he trying some kind of flanking maneuver?

Addya sped out of the trees and made for the nearest of the hills.

"There! That's her!"

The elevated pitch of the voice told her it was Iado's goons who'd spotted her, not the human.

Haven't heard or seen anything of him since the pistol went off. Once I lose Iado's thugs, I'll have to find him, make sure he didn't catch one of those bolts between the ears.

Her legs strained to push her up the hill and slow her descent down the other side. Keeping the cloak tucked around her, she crouched behind a hip-high bush. Her quick breathing sounded hollow in her own ears. She swallowed hard and forced herself to breathe through her nares with her beak closed. The extra noise of breathing through her mouth would draw attention before she was ready.

She drew her rapier and set it down next to her right hand. Then she pulled out the crossbow. A panel slid off the bottom of the stock. A handful of bolts as long as her fingers slid out. She set them aside and replaced the panel before drawing the string back and setting the first bolt into the groove.

Multiple voices and footsteps in the grass drew nearer, then drifted northward some, before turning back. Addya kept her crossbow aimed in their direction.

Iado's mob came toward her again.

"Surrender without any more fuss and maybe we'll kill you here instead of taking you back to the countess," Iado hollered.

Now there's an encouraging prospect.

Black feathers appeared at the top of the hill and bobbed in and out of sight while the guard worked his way up to the crest. As soon as she had a big enough target for her pathetic aim, she squeezed the trigger. The mini-crossbow made an almost cute-sounding thwack. She'd aimed right between his collarbones, but the bolt drove into the guard's shoulder.

Fine, so adjust my aim to the left.

The guard fell back.

Addya pulled the string back and loaded the next bolt into the groove as two guards reached the top of the rise. She aimed a bit left of one's chest and fired. He shrieked and dropped.

She loaded another bolt as the remaining three charged down the hill toward her. After squeezing off a shot that grazed Iado's arm, Addya dropped the crossbow and snatched up her sword. Two she could handle if they were the same caliber as the guards she'd faced at the countess's castle. Three might be a little much.

I don't suppose they'd be honorable enough to challenge me one at a time.

She swept the cloak back off her shoulders. The pressure of the closure against her throat was unpleasant but better than foiling her own blade work in yards of material. She backed up onto the slope behind her. The nearest of the guards charged in, shrieking wildly. Addya slapped his blade downward. The point stuck in the dirt. She hopped forward and lunged, driving the blade between his collarbones.

Iado stood at the bottom of the hill loading his full-sized crossbow while his remaining companion came at her. Her own crossbow was still at the base of the shrub where she'd left it. She'd have to get to Iado before he could fire. At the short distance between them, even a fledgling could hit the target.

As Addya crouched, a loud pop-bang half-deafened her. Iado yelped as the crossbow splintered in his hands. He clutched one wrist tightly in the other hand and fell to his knees.

A few yards in front of her, her remaining opponent jabbed the point of his rapier at her waist.

She parried it aside with a flick of her wrist. "Stand down. I do not enjoy killing."

"Give back those papers. Maybe I'll forget I saw you." The guard's eyes narrowed as he circled his way up the hill.

"Oh?" Addya snorted and adjusted her grip on

her sword. "You somehow got the papers and missed me? How would you explain that to your mistress? She doesn't strike me as the gullible type."

The guard straightened into the extended-arm starting position of the Aelstrian style, completely unsuited for this uneven ground. Addya instead crouched down into the human form. He took a couple steps toward her, coming out of the proper stance. Like the fledgling she'd fought in the narrow corridor, the guard's shoulders were too square to her. His whole torso made for an easy target.

Why can't you just go away? I've had enough of killing for this fortnight. She hissed.

The guard's eyes widened. "This is your last chance. Surrender, and you—"

Addya beat his blade aside and charged in. She grabbed his arm in one hand and planted the blade against his throat. "Do you drop your weapon or permanently give up breathing?"

The blade hit the grass and rolled downhill, but his other shoulder moved. She shoved him back and drew back with the sword. Something scraped across her leather tunic as he fell, dead before the ground caught him. A knife was clutched in his other hand. Her tunic had a fresh scrape from the point of the knife.

She glared at the corpse. "Idiot! I would have let you go home, or anywhere else you wanted as long as it was away from me!"

Grass rustled behind her. Addya tightened her hold on the rapier and whirled. Her cloak fell over her shoulders again, and she quickly shoved it back.

The blond human had left his horse somewhere

and now approached on foot. He had his rapier in one hand and pistol in the other, and there had been more than enough time for him to reload after shooting the crossbow out of Iado's hands.

Had he disabled Iado to help her or to collect whatever bounty Countess Yarek had offered?

Inches beyond Iado's reach, the human stopped. His narrow blue eyes studied her.

Karl watched the fifth black-feathered Aelstrian fall. The last, the one with the red beads in his crest, knelt nearby, rocking and holding one wrist tightly in the other hand.

The gray Aelstrian female spun toward him and pushed her cloak behind her shoulder. The beads in her crest whipped around and tapped her beak then swung back into place. Her quick breathing whistled softly through the nares on the top of her beak.

After watching how easily this one had eliminated five of the countess's men, Karl's heart thudded in his chest like a galloping horse's hooves.

Am I even half her skill?

He ordered his heart to slow back to the normal rhythm. His pistol would even out their abilities, if necessary.

She dug a dingy cloth from her pouch, revealing a brilliant blue interior, and wiped her blade clean. With well-practiced motions, she slid the blade into its sheath at her hip and then returned to the shrub where she'd discarded the mini-crossbow.

"Leave it." Karl tightened his hold on his pistol.

She glanced up at him and hissed. "Foolish creature. Do you think I drew Iado's attack away so I could kill you now? If I wanted you dead, I would have let you ride into Iado's force unaware. As it is, you slowed the task I have enough. Direct your gun at Iado. Yarek's chief guard is the one to watch, and watch also for the sixth one. I have only counted five. There were six to start."

"I shot one earlier when this whole chase started." He shifted more of his attention to Iado who still rocked and held his wrist.

She paused then gathered her bolts. "Unfortunate, however, they were not cordial creatures."

Her command of Schaflandish bore an ever-so-slight accent, carried mostly in the cadence of her words and the word choices she made to accommodate wrapping an inflexible beak around a human language.

"Your use of our language is excellent." He arched an eyebrow.

"Could I fill the role as well if I couldn't talk to you?" She opened a compartment on the crossbow and slipped the three remaining bolts inside. She gestured to Iado with a wave of her hand. "I need to get going. You have that one under control?"

"The only place you're going is back to Watcher Reiker with me."

She squinted at him. "Days do not exist for such a detour."

"Nevertheless, my lord insists, and you are in his

lands."

The gray bolted to her feet. Her feathers fluffed outward.

Karl stood his ground. "My lady, I have a feeling you've been much maligned. Your name needs clearing in my watcher's ears if nothing else. If your cause is just, he will not delay you for long."

"It is to your advantage that he does not." She smoothed her feathers and strutted over. "As the lord I act for does not wish hostilities with Schafland, I agree to go. I go only to honor those wishes."

"Fair enough."

Grabbing Iado by the uninjured arm, she hauled him to his feet and gave the graze on his arm and the apparently injured hand a cursory look. He squawked in protest and tried to shrug away from her.

Karl took Iado's rapier and crossbow bolts and led the way back to his horse.

As he slid his foot in the stirrup of his chestnut gelding's saddle, rough, taloned hands dragged him backward and threw him against the gray-plumed Aelstrian. They both fell back, and he landed squarely on top of her. The hilt of her rapier jabbed into his ribs.

Karl rolled to one side, got his feet under him, and grabbed his pistol. Iado disappeared into the tree line less than twenty feet away. After jogging several steps toward the forest, Karl fired at the shadow that might have been Iado. The ball hit with a loud thwack that came from a tree, not a body.

"I thought you had a good hold on him." He spun

back toward Pferd and the remaining Aelstrian.

She still lay on the ground. Her eyes squeezed shut then opened them, unable to focus on anything. A handful of black feathers were clutched in her hand.

He jogged back to her and crouched nearby. "What happened?"

"He fell, or at least he acted like he fell. When I tried to adjust the hold on him, he jerked away and reached for you." She rolled onto her side and pressed her scaly hand against the back of her head. "Are you hurt?"

"I think I'll get away with a couple bruises, but what about you?"

"Struck a rock and saw a constellation I share with no one else."

He leaned across her. "Let me see the damage."

She withdrew her hand. When he ran his fingers through her soft feathers, she winced and hissed. He sat back and found no blood on his fingers.

Just rattled your gourd a bit, most likely. "I don't see anything. Watcher Reiker's physician will know more." He offered his hands. "Think you can stand?"

"We can try." She clasped his wrists.

Her scaly fingers were smoother than he'd anticipated. She tucked her feet in closer and rolled up to a crouch. Continuing the movement, Karl rose, pulling her with him.

I've picked up kids who weigh more than you.

She stumbled against him when her balance betrayed her. Warm, fuzzy feathers brushed his bare face and neck.

Karl glanced back at his gelding. "Let's have Pferd do your walking until you feel steadier."

The gray's tail feathers fluttered as she swept the cloak to one side. "Horses are not easy to ride with a tail."

"You'll have to sit side-saddle." He guided her foot to the stirrup.

She hopped, and he lifted her up to Pferd's back. Eyes tightly clenched, she twisted around and sat sideways, with her cloak and tail off Pferd's opposite side.

Once she settled, she opened her eyes and blinked hard. "Ah, let us not do that again."

Karl walked around to the horse's other side and hauled himself up behind her. As little as she weighed, his gelding should be able to manage both of them.

He grabbed Pferd's reins and rode for the castle. The beads in her crest caught his eye. "You wear the royal blue."

"Clearly."

"Countess Yarek gave us a description of a fugitive that you match very well. She did not mention that you'd be wearing the royal blue."

She snorted. "Of course not, would that not raise curiosity?"

He nodded. "It would indeed. So, what's your side of this story?"

"I wish to tell that tale once only." She clicked her beak.

Karl frowned. "Can you at least tell me your name so I have something more appropriate to call you than 'You with the gray feathers?'"

"Safe enough, I think. Addya Dace."

"Karl Schildmann. Well met, and if I've forgotten my manners, thank you for the warning earlier."

"Sneak attacks are a coward's effort. Such things are disgusting. The cowardice is worse when the heraldry you wear is for an honorable creature."

"Why are you hiding your heraldry?"

She huffed. "I wish to tell–"

"–To tell that tale only once." Karl rolled his eyes. *This is going to be a long ride back.*

He urged his horse up to a canter.

Karl awoke with the sun. The campfire had dwindled to embers, which did little to discourage the chill of the morning air. Pferd, still tied to a nearby bush, nibbled on grass. On the far side of the fire, Addya roosted like a hen, her legs tucked under her and her beak under her left wing. Her courier pouch sat beside her.

After rebuilding the fire and saddling Pferd, he ate a modest breakfast of cheese and bread and stepped lightly over to the courier. He slipped the pouch's flap open. The color and royal crest marked her as a messenger of the king, but why was the rest of her clothing nondescript? There was something curious about this courier. There might be a reason for her to try to hide her credentials, but might she be the criminal Countess Yarek claimed?

The pouch contained typical traveling supplies: a water skin, some coins, flint and a striker, and other odds and ends. Curiously, there was no food. She'd either been traveling long enough to have exhausted her supply, or she'd had to leave suddenly enough to be unprepared. Some folded papers were tucked in a small pocket inside the pouch. Karl withdrew them and sat out of arm's reach.

The paper on top was a note of some sort, written in the odd wedges and swirls that made up Aelstria's written language. He recognized only a few words, not nearly enough to get the gist of the letter. The wax seal at the bottom showed a crown and two crossed scepters, obviously Countess Yarek's. The next was a four-column list. Two of the columns were words and the other two were numbers. Some of the words were names, and all the ones Karl recognized were nobility. The final paper was a map of Aelstria and Schafland, judging from the coastline and terrain features, but the boundaries were all wrong. Schafland had disappeared entirely. The king's name appeared nowhere on the map, but there were names of other nobility.

Karl spread out the map and the list side-by-side. With only two exceptions, the names in one column of the list were all on the map in various places. The names on the other side were missing. He thought back to the previous encounter with the courier in the red tunic. Someone was making an effort to oust the current king, which Watcher Reiker insisted would be bad for all of Schafland.

Which side was this courier on? Was she hiding her colors because she'd turned on the king? Then again, she'd agreed to speak to Reiker because her king would not approve of hostilities. If Yarek were chasing Addya, though, the bright tunic of a royal courier would be much more visible.

You're a spy for your king.

Addya awoke with the stony ground trying to burrow under her feathers. A fire beside her crackled and warmed her wing and back. Her headache had subsided from a pulse-tuned throbbing to a definite annoyance. Her sore backside didn't appreciate yesterday's ride and now rivaled her headache for the title of Most Aggravating Pain.

Paper crinkled behind her. Addya rose up into a crouch and turned toward the noise. Her headache spiked to somewhere near yesterday's intensity then dwindled back. Karl sat nearby with familiar papers laid out in front of him.

She pressed one hand to her head and reached for the papers with the other. "I did not take you for a thief."

"Forgive me." He refolded the papers and handed them back to her. "On one hand, I did not want to pry into your affairs. On the other, one of my duties is the safety of my people. You killed five with hardly an effort, and the countess says you've killed four others. Since you refused to speak of the reasons—"

"I killed only one other outright. The others were

alive when I left the area. I do not enjoy killing, regardless of what the countess suggested." She stuffed the papers back into her courier pouch and flipped the lid closed. "Can you read Aelstrian?"

"Not enough to read the notes, but that map made all clear, even without knowing the translation of the place names." He pointed to her pouch. "I saw the heraldry on the flap. You're a courier. That explains the blue."

"So it does, and at this instant, that title draws a target on these wings. It is essential for us all that the task I have is carried out with haste." She pushed off from the ground and came to her feet. The headache charged ahead then retreated. She winced. "Let us not allow the sun to rise further. If talking to Watcher Reiker is required, then let us leave now. I have no extra days."

He stood. "How is your head today?"

"It hurts. I will not slow us down."

"You don't weigh Pferd down much." He pointed to his already-saddled horse with his thumb. "He's strong enough to carry us both if we keep a reasonable pace."

She ruffled her tail. "These feathers have had enough of the saddle."

He chuckled. "I understand." Karl dug around in his saddlebag and offered her a hunk of bread and a piece of cheese. "Break your fast while I break camp."

She accepted the offered meal and paced around while she nibbled on pieces of it. The bread disintegrated into crumbs as she ate. Some enterprising ants would have a grand time tracing her path around the campsite. The cheese held together better, and between them, they made for a sufficient meal. While she ate, Karl used a small shovel to separate the remaining wood in the fire and to pile rocky dirt on the whole business. She finished before he did and secured his rolled-up blanket to his saddle.

Once the fire was properly out, he secured the saddlebags and pulled himself up into the saddle.

Karl offered her his hand. "Are you sure you won't try the saddle a little longer? We'll travel faster."

"You have not seen Aelstrians travel on foot? On uneven terrain?" She ruffled her feathers and broke into a nice jog.

At the crest of the hills, she spread her wings and launched, gliding dozens of yards before the increasing drag and decreasing velocity returned her to earth. Each landing shot pain across the back of her head, but that slowed her down only slightly. The sooner she finished this ridiculous audience, the sooner she could be back on her way.

The horse's hooves clopped over the stones and dirt as Karl caught up to her.

10

Addya sat in the study of Watcher Reiker. The room was decorated in the simple elegance of well-polished woods and shelves piled with books and personal treasures, a stark change from Countess Yarek's jeweled and embroidered crimson and black.

Karl, still clad in his dusty riding clothes, stood with his lord near the shelves. The older human was tall and thin for his race. His brown doublet and trousers had no more ostentation than the furnishings.

She sat still and let the human physician turn her head feathers into a ruffled mess. The pressure of his fat fingers probing around the back of her head elicited a shrieking pain. She winced and jerked away from him.

"That's the spot, eh? Mmhm. No broken skin at least." He walked around and sat facing her. "And the headache has been constant ever since?"

"Yes, I said that already." *Pay attention, human. I have no time to repeat myself.*

"Any other symptoms? Queasiness? Sleeplessness? Dizziness? Is light or noise bothersome?"

"At first, yes. Not now." She turned a narrow gaze on him. "I said all this once, too."

He nodded. "Add irritable to the symptom list."

"Only since you delay the task I have."

The physician sighed and tapped his cheek. "I'd say you likely have a concussion. You really should rest for a few days, at least until that headache fades."

"Rest a few days?" She pushed herself up and shuffled to the window. "Not a good idea."

Humans milled around the courtyard tending to livestock and fetching objects from one end of the bailey to the other. They behaved as if today were like yesterday and yesterday were like tomorrow. Didn't they know how precarious their position was? They could be enslaved or dead by this time next month if Countess Yarek had her way.

She shook her head and turned back to the physician. "There aren't a few days in the schedule. The longer I stay, the worse it is. This delay in the travel is too great even now. None of you realize the danger you are in."

"I'm not sure you realize the danger you're in, young lady." The physician wagged his finger at her. "Head injuries are not to be trifled with. Without proper rest, you could really do yourself some mischief."

Watcher Reiker's boots clacked loud-soft, loud-soft on the wooden floor as he came forward. "Thank you, Doctor."

"Certainly, sir, but see if you can talk some sense into this young chick." The physician sighed and left, closing the door behind him.

Reiker gestured to the simple table and chairs near his desk. "Please be seated, both of you. Can I get you anything to drink, Addya?" He went to a tea service a servant had left on one of the shelves.

Addya turned a chair sideways and sat facing the table. "Water is fine, thank you."

He joined them with a shallow bowl of water and two steaming cups of brown liquid. She lapped up a few swallows of the water while the gentlemen sipped their drinks.

Reiker set his cup down. "Now, where were we before the doctor arrived?" He studied the ceiling for a moment before his eyes widened. "Yes. Now I remember. You found evidence of the countess' betrayal, along with half the other nobility, and your intention is to complete this trek across half the peninsula to get the evidence to the king."

"Yes, and sooner is advantageous." Addya set the bowl down. "Vital now that Iado got away. He will go directly to his countess to testify that I yet live. I gave away two days already to answer your request. I do not want to lose the rest."

"Forgive me for asking the obvious, but–" Karl scratched his short beard and frowned. "Why must you personally be the one to deliver the evidence to your king?"

She narrowed her eyes and leaned toward him. "I was charged with this task and see no reason I should leave it undone."

Reiker shook his head. "I've been Watcher for many years, and I have never approved of a trusted agent risking his, or her, life unnecessarily for such a reason. You're more useful to your king alive than dead, are you not?"

She hissed but swallowed the sharp answer

building in her head. *Am I being hard-headed just to be hard-headed? Evryt would not want me dead. He said as much when he agreed to let me have this job.* "Yes, you are right. We all cease to be useful when we die."

"Precisely. So driving yourself to an early grave for the sake of duty is fruitless when it's avoidable." Reiker crossed one arm over his belly, rested his opposite elbow on that arm and his chin on his fingers. "From the demands Yarek made on us and the place where you and Karl encountered her guards, the countess wants you specifically, and she expects you to follow a route directly from here to the Aelstrian capital." He pointed in the general direction of the palace. "Subterfuge on our part would be prudent."

Her feathers flared outward. "So you suggest that I should reject du–" *Yes, and with good reason.* She clenched her beak and then blew a deep breath out of her nares. *Hear him out. Maybe the idea isn't all bad.* "What do you have in your thoughts?"

He sat up straighter. "Prepare a message. I have paper and ink you can use. Include the pertinent information and a promise of direct evidence as soon as you can get there. Code it however you wish. Make a few copies. I'll send one with some of my men by the most direct route." He numbered off ideas on his fingers. "One can go with a trade caravan preparing to leave in the morning. One can go with my own courier to Lord Quetik in the north. According to your information, he's still loyal, and he's in a much better position to begin preparations to repel an insurrection. Yarek clearly doesn't have favorable thoughts toward us, so I'll also alert my own capital and the other nobility in Schafland. In the meantime, you rest here until your injuries heal then leave under some kind of disguise either to Lixine or to Quetik as seems most prudent when the time comes."

Karl nodded. "The countess will likely ignore those other messengers in a desperate hunt for you. Either way, the message will likely reach the king. The papers should also go with one of these messengers and for the same reasons. We can split the papers among the different messengers to ensure at least one reaches the king. Any of them would be sufficient evidence to depose the countess."

She stood up and walked to the window. The dull headache surged, pulsing with her heartbeat until it receded to an annoyance seconds later.

The suggestion sounded reasonable enough. Sending a vital message by multiple couriers was a standard practice.

Which is more important, my agitated nerves or getting the critical information to the king?

The old human joined her at the window. "At the very least, you increase the chances of getting the information through with no risk of aggravating injuries."

"Very well." She turned to face him directly. "I do not like to sit on my tail when there is critical work. Still, if the countess searches for these feathers, others can get through where I cannot."

The watcher smiled and pointed to his desk. "Excellent. Use my writing set."

The chair had arms. Addya spun the chair sideways and perched on the arm.

Countess Talia Yarek sat in the basket of her balloon and preened her feathers while Captain Iado perched on the floor nearby polishing his blade, his fifth issued from the armory just in the last year. The missing clump of feathers on one arm gave him a rather scruffy appearance, and the bandage tied around the other didn't help.

Her airship descended in a tight spiral.

A maid knelt next to her. "We'll be landing momentarily."

She opened her beak to cue the guards, but all six lined up near the door to announce her arrival before she could issue her orders. Iado stayed in his place. Until that bandaged arm recovered and he regrew the missing feathers, he would not be appropriate for her honor guard. He was only here because after so many years of service, he deserved at least a chance to even the debt with that infernal courier and the human sheriff.

The airship settled with a jolt and a thud.

Talia clicked her beak and squinted in the direction of the driver's platform above her. *He simply must learn to land this thing without rattling us all to pieces.*

The guard in front of the door threw it opened and all six jogged out to their places. As soon as they started the announcement with their twenty-second trill, Talia began counting their timing. The first two blades clashed almost six seconds too early.

She ground her bottom beak against the top one. *They'll be practicing that again for certain. Of course, with those first two off, the rest will be incorrect as well.*

As predicted, the next two sets were off their pace. She rolled her eyes and waited for silence before strutting through the door and under the sword-arch. Watcher Hans Reiker stepped out of the main building and closed the door behind him. The old man wore his usual dull, peasant-like doublet and trousers. His rapier hung from the left side of his belt.

Talia huffed. What use was making a grand entrance if her intended audience hadn't even been there to watch? At least he hadn't observed her honor guard's most embarrassing gaffe.

Reiker took a few steps forward but stopped well short of the sword-arch. "Countess, I didn't expect you back here so soon."

"Your sheriff ca'tured the fugitive, did he not?" She joined him and drilled a narrow-eyed stare through his forehead.

"I told you I would send for you, or send the fugitive to you, at the appropriate time." His hand rested on the hilt of his sword.

"I'll take her and what she stole now."

"I don't think so."

"Really?" She whistled a high, steady note.

Equipment and feathers rustled. Shadows in her peripheral vision grew larger as her honor guard formed a shoulder-to-shoulder line behind her.

Reiker propped both hands on his hips. "I am not your vassal, and I will not accept orders from you."

He raised one hand and made an abrupt forward motion. Men from all over the courtyard dropped whatever they were carrying and rushed to form a barricade around the side of the airship where the honor guard and main door were. Steel rasped on leather as the men drew swords or knives. The men directly in front held flintlock pistols at the ready.

Reiker stepped back behind the line. "I would seriously reconsider your choices, Countess. Just my on-duty staff outnumbers your entire crew for that airship. I would suggest you stop this charade and leave with all haste. This time, head for your own border with your entire staff instead of letting a handful off to invade my countryside."

"Your guards." She snorted and squinted at Reiker. "Any one of these feathers is good for any five of yours."

"If they can get that far, you would still be outnumbered. Try your hand if you feel the need. Just remember that you're in the front with a half-dozen of my best marksmen aiming at your head."

Talia's eyes narrowed. Clearly, Addya had already spoken to the old man and revealed the evidence. The damage had been done most effectively. What would the best course of action be now? A melee battle here would accomplish nothing. Her group would undoubtedly kill many of Reiker's men before falling themselves to superior numbers, and then who would fly her airship? Most likely, Addya was already on her way to that frightfully young upstart calling himself the king. There wasn't much time.

"Well, Countess? What will your decision be?" Reiker asked.

Count Zyrus Quetik was in the best position to oppose the coup. If she played her cards right, she could eliminate him before he could get the proper warning.

Talia hissed at Reiker. "I leave 'ecause it suits 'e. Know with certainty, Reiker, I will recall this affront of yours. You will wish you had not crossed 'e."

She pivoted on one foot and strutted back to her airship. The guards followed. The last one aboard closed and secured the door.

She glared in the direction of the old man and muttered in her own language, "I have half a mind to drop a few incendiaries on his head."

"We have them aboard," Iado replied.

"We may need them for Quetik." She turned to her captain, still polishing his sword. "That's enough of that. You have an assault to plan."

Iado's eyes widened. "An assault, with just the seven of us?"

"Find a way." *Or be finished as my guard captain.*

He beckoned all the guards over.

Talia waddled to one of the windows and lifted the flap. The terrain spiraled smaller and smaller as the airship lifted off. Reiker's people had dispersed and the man himself had gone inside. She searched the countryside. Finding the courier's blue would be impossible. Iado's report was that she'd traded the standard tunic for a better camouflaged cloak and tunic. Tree cover in this part of Schafland was minimal, so a tan and gray figure moving toward the capital shouldn't be too hard to spot, but nothing below moved.

As the airship wheeled around, a long, interrupted stripe of white caught her eye. She squinted into the distance. A series of covered wagons and humans on horseback traveled toward Reiker's castle. A merchant caravan wasn't likely to stay in one place for long. Maybe a suitable offer of reward would convince them to keep an eye out for the courier. She went aft to signal the pilot.

Addya blinked hard. She hissed and squinted.

Mmhm. I couldn't see straight the last time I knocked my head, either. And you wanted to continue traveling? Karl perched on the side of the desk. "Perhaps it would be better if you tell me what to write. If there's no one at court who can read Schaflandish, then the courier can do the job and someone can translate his words."

"I can see well enough." She dipped the pen into the ink. "Should you not guard your watcher?"

"At present, your defensive abilities are compromised. There are others who can protect him very well. Over half of those 'peasants' out there are guards or militiamen in disguise. Trouble was anticipated after the countess' last visit."

"Wise." Addya drew the final marks on the first

letter and set it aside. "That one is for the count. Just the ones for the king now."

She slid another paper over and wrote a greeting, but the format of the letter was simpler.

Karl leaned over to look at the paper. "Hmm. Interesting. If you don't mind my asking, what is your connection with the king?"

"Why do you think there is one?" She dipped the pen in the ink and continued.

"I can't read Aelstrian, but I know the difference between a formal letter and an informal one." Karl tapped the corner of the paper. "This is an informal one." He pointed to the finished letter to Count Quetik. "That one is formal. That suggests you have a connection to the king stronger than employer and worker. A childhood friend? Relative, perhaps?"

"Is it vital?"

"Not really, but it would help me understand what's driving you so hard. I get the distinct impression there's more than duty involved. You're genuinely worried."

She snorted. "I do not see why you cannot know. It is no secret. Ji–"

The door opened, and Wolfgang stepped into the room. The lad barely stood hip-high and wore his page's sash slightly askew. "Sir?"

Karl stood. "Go ahead, lad. What's the word?"

"The chatelaine says that the room in the southwest corner has been prepared for the courier when she's ready. It should be quietest."

Karl frowned. "It'll get evening sun."

"Yes, sir. She's added an extra drape to the curtain to block the sun."

"Good thinking. Thank you." Karl sat on the edge of the desk as the boy left. "Your relationship to the king?"

Addya hissed at the paper and crossed out a group of symbols. "Jianna is a childhood friend. Evryt is a cousin. They encounter each other only due to knowing these feathers together."

"Yes, that clarifies everything. With such ties, Yarek would be unlikely to purchase your loyalty."

"Even in your history, the worst traitors were related to the ruler they turned on." She paused and glanced up at him before going back to the letter.

"True, but rarely a relative and a friend."

"The countess is not interested in offering her own wealth to acquire loyalty. She could not get the loyalty of these feathers for all the wealth she owns and knows it." She signed off at the bottom of the letter.

"And this whole insurrection is because the king is in the wrong family line?"

Addya wrote an informal heading. "Yes. If not for the crown going to a younger son two generations ago, Countess Yarek would have the throne now, and we would have war."

"So, if she eliminates the current king, he has no heir, so the throne passes to her." Karl nodded and studied the courier. "But you're a cousin to the king."

"These feathers are the third in the succession, at least until Jianna hatches an egg. I have no interest in the throne. Evryt can have it with the great joy of these feathers." Addya set the pen down and rubbed her eyes for a moment.

Karl reached for the paper she was working on.

"If it's a copy of the last–"

She swatted his hand away. "I can do it."

The door opened with a slight squeak of the hinge.

Watcher Reiker closed it after him. "Countess Yarek is gone for the moment."

Karl stood. "What was it about?"

"More useless posturing and demands. The usual fare with that one." He waved the topic away with a sweep of his hand. "Curious thing, though. She took off to the north."

Addya's head snapped up. She winced. "Toward Count Quetik's territory."

"She could yet veer off." Reiker brought a chair over from the table. "She might simply be on the hunt for you."

Addya set her current letter aside and picked up the first one again. She added a postscript. "I doubt that. Iado has had long enough to reach her. She was here seeking these feathers, was she not?"

"She was at that, and rather adamantly, too. If it wouldn't guarantee war, I'd have arrested her and her crew."

She finished writing and handed the letter over. "For the count, and he needs it as soon as a rider can travel there."

"Once the countess is out of visual range, I'll send my best riders on their fastest horses." Reiker settled into the chair and read the letter.

Karl picked up the second letter. "This is the first one for the king. She's on the second now. Then there's just the one for the caravan due tonight."

"No need for the last. I will leave with the

caravan." Addya set the pen aside.

Reiker frowned. "What happened to getting the rest you need?"

"The countess changed everything." Addya pressed her scaly, gray fingers against her head. "I can rest on the way in one of the wagons."

Reiker leaned forward. "Why this renewed hurry?"

Karl slid the paper back in front of Addya and offered her the pen. "She's kin of the king and friend of the queen."

"If the countess gave in without a fight, she left too easily." She huffed and took the pen but didn't resume the letter writing.

"She was in a bit of a bind." Reiker glanced back toward the courtyard. "She was surrounded and had no fewer than six pistols aimed directly at her own skull."

"She threw grenades at you as she left?"

"No."

"Too easy. She has a scheme in the works. She's not finished yet. If she is not going after Count Quetik, she is after reinforcements."

"I have a couple lads who volunteered to follow the airship back to the border and report back," Reiker said.

"They know to stay out of throwing range?" Addya asked.

"They do indeed." Reiker nodded toward the paper. "Now, finish that letter so you can get your rest. We'll see how you feel when the caravan is ready to depart tomorrow."

Karl watched over Addya's shoulder while she

wrote. He understood her concern, certainly, but a concussion would need more than a good night's rest and a decent meal to overcome.

The hinge creak that jolted Karl from sleep belonged only to the jail cell door. A jail break? Barefoot and in his nightshirt, he grabbed his pistol from the peg on the wall and darted out the front door. That rascal of a messenger was sprinting toward the main doors of the keep. The guards on duty there stepped away from the doors and drew their swords. The messenger hissed and changed course for the stone wall surrounding the castle.

"Stop!" Karl ordered.

The messenger kept running as Friedhelm, the night watchman, darted out of the guardhouse. His dog, Schnauzen, barked like a netherworld hound on a mission.

Friedhelm unsnapped the leash. "Pin 'im down, Schnauzen!"

The dog took off as if launched from an arbalest and tackled the messenger ten feet away from the wall. Schnauzen stood with his front paws on the messenger's shoulders and continued barking.

The messenger shrieked. "Off! Off!"

Karl jogged closer but waited for Friedhelm to saunter over.

"Off!" The messenger tried to push off but gave up as the barking continued.

"Stay still." Karl stopped a few feet back. "He'll follow his orders, but don't rile him up any further by trying to get away."

Friedhelm caught the dog by the collar. "Out, Schnauzen."

The dog backed off and growled.

Before moving in, Karl waited for the night watchman's nod. Schnauzen knew everyone who belonged to the castle, but a healthy respect for those teeth was always warranted.

Karl caught the messenger by the arm and hauled him up. His legs buckled under him, and Karl tightened his grip. "What's this about? What were you hoping to do? Kill the watcher? The Courier?"

"Either. 'Oth. Neither." The messenger hissed and tried to jerk free until another heartfelt bark from Schnauzen cut that effort short. "What do you care?"

The keep doors opened and the Courier darted out, sword at the ready. She slowed and approached at a steady, measured pace.

Karl frowned. *What are you doing out of bed?*

"There are few creatures I regret leaving alive, you stain on Aelstrian dignity." Addya's eyes narrowed.

The messenger hissed and shrieked at Addya, continuing on in their own language for some time.

She snorted. "Even if I were the sort to kill you now, you are in the care of Watcher Reiker. Insulting these feathers or Evryt's will not change that. I would only grant your request at the watcher's order."

"Let's go." Karl pulled the messenger with him

and turned to the dog handler. "Thank you, Friedhelm. Schnauzen definitely earned his feed this night."

"That he did, sir." Friedhelm ruffled the fur on his dog's head and led him away.

Halfway back to the jail, the messenger twisted around, aiming his talons at Karl's face. As Karl flinched away from the strike, Addya stepped in. The messenger backhanded her across the beak, and a moment later, a hard kick against the back of the knees sent Karl to the ground hard. The messenger knelt over him. Sharp talons scratched his hand, and a heartbeat later, his own pistol was aimed at his chest. Karl shoved, taking advantage of his greater mass, and dislodged the messenger. The gun fired with a pop of the charge in the frizzen. Karl rolled aside before the bang of the main charge as a shriek came from one of the Aelstrians. Karl scrambled back to his feet. Addya's sword came through the messenger's chest.

She caught him and lowered him to the ground, as if he were a comrade, not an adversary. "Foolish. You could have gotten the law's grace."

The Aelstrian answered in his own language and died.

Addya withdrew her sword. "He fell toward me. I could not dodge quickly enough."

"This isn't your fault, Addya." He offered his hand and pulled her up. "He wanted you to kill him, didn't he?"

"Yes." She blew a deep breath out through her nares. "The Countess gave two choices: recover the evidence or face the watcher's justice. He could not get the evidence and could not consider death at the hands of a Schaflander."

He gripped her shoulder. "Get some rest and try not to think about this. You did nothing wrong."

She took her eyes off the messenger's corpse. "You are hurt?"

"A scratch or two, nothing more. How's your head."

"It hurts. I will live." She nodded and walked back toward the keep.

He watched her leave then sent someone for the undertaker.

11

Karl stroked the horse's shoulder and checked the harness. Satisfied it was secure and set properly to avoid injuring the horse, he darted back to the wagon. Planting both hands on the wagon's floor, he jumped and pushed himself up. The inside of this wagon had crates lined up along the floor and baskets to one side. The pile of blankets he'd brought from the keep would become a passable bed for the resting courier.

The back of the wagon jiggled. Karl twisted around as Reiker climbed up.

"Is everything arranged with the caravan leader?" Karl asked.

Reiker nodded but frowned. "Better than I expected, actually. He didn't offer much of a fight at all. I told him who the passenger would be, and he immediately agreed. I thought that was rather odd."

Karl stretched a blanket out on the crates and folded it double. "That is odd. This is the same caravan leader who balked at taking a satchel to the capital last month?"

"Yes, because he'd lose cargo room, but he had no problem with dedicating half of this wagon to a bed for an Aelstrian courier. I'd almost rather he'd been a bit fussier. Now I wonder what has changed."

"I'll keep my eyes open." He spread out another

blanket.

Reiker handed over the next blanket. "I wish our courier would reconsider this trip. I don't like it."

"She won't, but I'll keep an eye on her, too."

"Karl." Reiker rested his hand on Karl's shoulder. "Are you all right with this assignment? I can send another."

He drew a deep breath. "I'm all right. I can't say that I have much trust for Aelstrians in general, but this one – this one's dedicated and if she meant harm to any of us, she had opportunity and didn't use it. Even when she's attacked, she tries to avoid killing."

"Yes, I heard about last night. A pity about how that turned out, but you both acted admirably. I'll send for her and find out if she's up for the trip."

As he hopped down from the wagon, Karl resumed arranging a bed.

Addya awoke with a dull ache in her head and surveyed the room. Her night-adjusted eyes did a fine job of providing her with the layout. The firm bed and plain, white quilt had given her a very restful night. The well-sanded wood of the furniture had no decorative carving or swirls. Very utilitarian, like everything else in Reiker's home.

What's the hour? Addya turned to the window.

The heavy curtains were dark. She shrugged off the covers and shivered in the cooler air. Fluffing out her feathers for warmth, she rose. The perpetual headache of the last few days surged ahead to shrieking pain. She grabbed the headboard with one hand and pressed the other to her head until the pain dwindled back down.

No sudden movements for me.

Addya walked to the window and pulled the curtain aside. Her vision hadn't cleared much, but she could discern a flock of stars against the black sky. The edge of the horizon glowed a rosy pink.

Perfect timing. She shook out her feathers and bobbed her head once.

Addya let the drapes close and pulled on her tunic. The buttons on the heavy garment weren't quite as stiff as when she'd first received it, but she still had to argue with the second one to get it into the hole. After getting those fastened, she belted on her rapier, slipped her courier pouch over her shoulder, and flicked the cloak around her shoulders.

She stepped lightly to the door. The knob twisted without a squeak, but that hinge had awakened the whole castle last night. Perhaps a slower movement would reduce the noise. The hinge made up for knob's silence with a squeal that would announce her intentions as far away as the next continent. As soon as there was enough room to squeeze through, Addya hissed at the noisy door and slipped through to the hallway.

The light taps of her toe talons on the bare wooden floor sounded like cannon shots. She made her way to the stairs, which might as well have been a mile to the ground floor. She gripped the handrail on the way down.

Moving slowly and carefully, she avoided the explosions that had racked her skull the previous night.

Addya turned right. After a few dozen feet, the surroundings became more familiar. The kitchen where they'd eaten lunch yesterday was off to the right down one corridor. The left hallway opposite led to the study. From there, she passed into the main foyer.

The front door flew open. Addya jumped and drew her rapier. She stood erect with her sword at shoulder height and aimed toward the source of trouble.

One of the little boys Reiker used for messengers skidded to a stop and fell backwards. He screamed and scrambled toward the door, hitting the door frame with his shoulder. Addya flinched. She sheathed her sword and stepped away. A heavy-set man arrived in seconds and pulled the boy out of the door. The man entered brandishing an ax.

Addya showed both hands empty and made the mental switch to the human's language. "He startled these feathers. I drew the sword I carry and scared the lad. I intend no injury."

"Courier?" The man came a step closer and squinted.

"Yes." She showed him the bright blue of her pouch.

He heaved a sigh, lowered the ax, and turned to the messenger. "Boy, how many times you been told not to throw the door open like that. You're going to hit someone or get hit yourself. Now dry your face.

You're not hurt. Finish your errand." He walked off mumbling.

The boy sniffled and wiped his nose on his sleeve. He shuffled closer and kept his eyes on the floor except for an occasional glance up at her. "Watcher Reiker sent me to ask if you wanted to rest here or leave with the caravan."

"They leave this early?"

"Yes, m'lady. Always before sunrise. The caravan leader likes to leave early."

"Clearly." Addya slipped out the door.

Two long rows of canvas-covered wagons filled the courtyard. In the dull pre-dawn light, humans hurried around with the help of lanterns. The watcher himself stood behind the rearmost wagon on the right with his head poked in through the canvas curtain hanging across the back.

So much for sneaking away early. She looked down at the boy. "I will leave with the caravan."

He nodded once and ran out.

Addya closed the door behind her and followed. The messenger got to Reiker first and pointed back at her while he spoke.

The curtain opened and Karl hopped down from the back of the wagon. He waved her over.

She walked toward them, trying to keep her movements as even and calm as she could.

"You're up early." Reiker glanced toward the dawn sky.

Addya took in the whole caravan with the wave of her hand. "So are others."

Reiker blew out a breath. "I wish you'd stay here until you're properly healed, but I understand your priorities. Let us pray for a safe and uneventful journey for you all."

"Thank you for all your assistance. I will certainly tell Evryt."

A man somewhere behind Addya called for the watcher.

Reiker looked past her and waved. "Stop by again if you cross this way."

Once he'd gone, Karl offered his hand up into the back, but she grabbed the edge and hauled herself upward. Her skull gave her a stern rebuke. Addya groaned, sank to her knees, and squeezed her eyes closed.

The back of the wagon jiggled and a steadying hand pressed on her shoulder.

"You're going to have to be more careful for a while," Karl scolded.

Addya hissed. "I hate injuries."

"I'm not enamored of them myself, but they heal more quickly if you give them time." He pulled her up and guided her to a padded surface. "Here. I've set up a bed for you. Lie down and sleep if you can. We'll be getting under way shortly."

She let him set her cloak and weapons aside but kept a firm hold on the courier pouch. She roosted with her legs under her, tucked her beak under her wing, and closed her eyes.

Karl guided his gelding around the outer perimeter of the ring of wagons. The sun had set a couple hours ago, but the moonlight showed the shrubbery and scraggly oaks as blobs and crooked spindles in the landscape of low, rolling hills.

As he neared the caravan master's wagon, the old man stepped out and walked over. "Better get some sleep, sheriff. Morning doesn't come any slower on the trail than it does in the keep."

Karl reined Pferd in and leaned forward in the saddle. "Just making my final rounds. Old habits and so forth."

"Sentries will alert us if anyone suspicious comes near." The caravan master indicated the camp with a nod.

"I'll just finish this circuit and then turn in."

"Right. See you at dawn, then."

Karl waited until the old man was safely back in his wagon before continuing on. The uneven terrain around the keep leveled out considerably a day's ride away, but the lower hills could still camouflage a sizable force, particularly in the dark. Near a convenient hilltop, he stopped and listened for movement or rattling equipment. Bugs chirped and the wind blew, but no sounds suggested humans or Aelstrians were in the area.

He turned back toward the wagons. Ahead, flickering candlelight from within one cast shadows of two men on the canvas. There was the low rustle of the pair talking, but the distance garbled the words until he rode closer.

"And once they're gone, we'll be five thousand richer!" The younger one giggled.

A loud whack stopped the giggling. "Let the whole camp in on it, why don't you? He's around somewhere, and you know what they say about those birds. They hear everything."

Karl moved Pferd on using what remained of the conversation to cover his departure. *That's the problem with these caravans. You never know who their employer really is.*

He cut across the camp to his own wagon and stepped from Pferd's saddle into the back. Addya's eyes beamed red eye-shine at him.

"It's me," he whispered. He gathered up Pferd's saddle bags and Addya's cloak and passed her rapier to her. "We have to go."

"Why?" She sheathed a knife.

"A couple men are plotting our demise."

The red eye-shine narrowed to stripes. "Are these not Reiker's—"

"No. They're professional merchants. They buy their goods from us, travel to the destination, and sell everything and hope for a good profit. We're just tagging along."

Addya tossed off the light blanket covering her and came up to a crouch. Karl stepped out of the back of the wagon and secured the saddle bags to Pferd's back. Addya pushed the curtain open. He offered her a hand down. Unlike this morning, she clasped his hand and planted the other on his shoulder and stepped down.

"How well can you see in the dark?" he asked.

"Once these eyes adjust to the darkness, I see details well, not colors. A little greater accuracy than you."

"Good." He gestured Addya on ahead of him. "Let's get away from here, set our own camp, and then determine what to do next."

After glancing back at the circle of wagons, he led Pferd by the reins and jogged to catch up with Addya. He let her set the pace and hustled to stay with her. A shout from the camp brought a clamoring and more voices. Karl pulled himself up into the saddle and offered Addya a hand. Kicking off from the ground she swung up behind him, hissing lightly.

Uncertain of the terrain, he didn't want to risk a full gallop in the dark, but he pushed Pferd as much as he dared and headed for a dense collection of oak trees.

Addya gripped his shoulder in a firm, but not painful hold. "They follow on foot. Looks like a dozen Schaflanders with torches, lanterns, and swords."

"They may be circling." He stayed focused on the terrain ahead of them. "We're going to get to that stand of trees ahead and take advantage of our dark colors."

"Greater effectiveness for your idea if we leave the first stand and continue with that one hindering the view of our hunters."

He nodded. "If there is a suitable stand of trees beyond the first, we'll do that."

Passing the first copse, he turned slightly to interpose the trees between them and the pursuers. Ahead, there was another stand of trees, but not quite so dense. Still, if they could get there, get Pferd down, and become part of the terrain before the men from the caravan caught up, they might get out of this without a fight.

Karl slowed Pferd as they approached the

second stand of trees. He dismounted and helped Addya down before threading his way around the trunks. The oaks grew at the top of a shallow rise.

At the lowest point, Karl lifted Pferd's nearer front foot and tugged the opposite rein. "Down. Down."

The gelding, breathing hard after carrying two riders at such a speed, huffed and turned but stayed on his feet. The torchlight visible through the further trees came closer.

He patted Pferd's neck. "I know this isn't the best situation. Down." He tugged the rein harder.

Pferd knelt on his front legs, then flopped down, but with his head still up, he would continue showing a definite horse profile. There wasn't time to get Pferd to lie flat. Karl crouched near his horse's neck to break up the line. Pferd's hot breath was loud enough to give them away. The clamoring of the crowd came nearer from the direction they'd traveled, and hoof beats echoed from a different direction.

"You were right. They flanked us," Addya whispered.

Karl looked in the direction of the voice but couldn't spot the courier. *Great camouflage.* "Stay still; stay quiet."

No answer returned. They waited, and Karl's legs protested being in that crouched position, but he didn't dare move. Gradually, Pferd's breathing slowed and quieted.

The hoof beats approached fastest and stopped a stone-throw away. Another set approached from a different direction.

"Did you find them?" a nasally voice asked.

"Not that way. You?"

"Would I have asked you if I had?"

"Hey, don't get smart with me."

"Maybe you need to get smart yourself."

"Stow it, both of you. Fan out and search the area," a third, deeper voice ordered.

"In the dark? What are we going to see in this light? Lucky I didn't find a chuck hole and break my fool neck galloping around out here."

"Yeah, or a snake."

"Just do as you're told."

"Where you going?"

"To tell Norbert. Search for them and return to camp. Remember. We only get paid for this extra job if we deliver."

One set of hoof beats retreated toward the torch-bearing crowd just arriving at the first stand of trees.

"'Just do as you're told,'" the nasally voice mocked. "Pfff. See what power will do for you?"

The other man snorted. "You rather tell Norbert we just let five thousand per man get away from us? Come on. Let's find them."

"Can't see a thing out here."

"Yeah? So hunt for something that resembles two riders on one horse. Otherwise, we'd better check some of the denser trees where they might hide."

"Starting with that one?"

"Who'd hide there? Dense trees. Shrubs. Y'know, something you could hide a horse behind. I don't think that scrawny bird courier could hide in those trees. There's not enough of them."

The two horsemen wandered a bit, closer and further. The real hazard, the torch-bearers, thoroughly checked out the denser first copse but didn't come much closer. Karl's leg muscles trembled but he clenched his jaw and stayed still. The chill in the air pierced his clothes, bringing another source of quivering. Finally, the hoof beats retreated, and the crowd left.

Karl stood and stretched his sore leg muscles before he tugged Pferd's reins. "Up."

As Pferd awkwardly regained his feet, Addya stood and pressed her hand to her head. "So, where now? If we shadow the caravan, we risk discovery, and the quantity of creatures involved in the search gives odds I do not care for. If we travel all night–"

"No." He joined her. "We could get ahead of them, but based on what little Watcher Reiker told the caravan about your mission, they would expect us to do exactly that. Pferd can carry us both, but not at a gallop for long, and they have some good horses in that caravan. They could send riders to overtake us. Better, I think to–"

Addya held up her hand, drawing her rapier. She staggered a step but reached a hand out to check her balance.

He rose and drew his own sword. "What did you hear?"

"A creature near at hand. I cannot tell what." She pointed toward the brush a dozen steps away.

Karl passed her Pferd's reins. "Hang onto him for me."

He moved between her and the sound and slunk forward. The hair on the back of his neck rose and his guts unsettled.

A deep growl came from the shrubs.

"Wolf?" Addya asked.

"Maybe. Ready your crossbow." Karl scanned from side to side, lingering on the denser parts of the brush where someone might be hiding.

Behind him, equipment rattled. The small weapon creaked.

The growl turned into barking deep enough to be a formidable dog. Karl stopped.

A distant door squeaked. "Teer! Get over here before you wake the whole province. Come on, Teer."

The barking changed from a low rumbling bark to a somewhat higher pitched sound that retreated.

Karl sheathed his sword and returned to Addya and Pferd. "Let's ask about bunking in their barn. It still gets chilly in the morning and a fire will give us away to the caravan."

He took Pferd's reins and led the way around the clump of brush and up the shallow hill to the flat land around the house. Out of the depression and the shrubbery, the wind pierced his cloak. Addya's head feathers fluffed up.

About fifty yards ahead, firelight glowed through the windows of a stone and wood farmhouse surrounded by a knee-high border of small rocks. The smell of burning wood carried on the air. The rippled field between them and the house was overgrown with short grasses and the stubble left from the recent harvest.

Karl listened for movement. The wind rustled through the grasses, weeds, and shrubs, but no equipment jingled. While they crossed the open field, he scanned from one side to the other. Barking came from inside the house. He stopped at the edge of the fence. Another dozen yards separated them from the door.

Addya snorted. "That dog sounds huge."

"That's why we're not going any closer without the owner's permission." He cupped his hands around his mouth. "Hello!"

The dog's barking continued, and paws scraped the inside of the door.

"Down, Teer!" The man's voice sounded muffled through the door. "Elsa, hang on to him, will you?"

The door creaked open.

A backlit silhouette of a lean man stood in the opening. "And who are you?"

"I'm Sheriff Karl Schildmann. I'm traveling with an Aelstrian lady. We were—"

"The sheriff, Otto? Is he here about the injured lad?" A woman called from inside.

Karl glanced back at Addya. "Injured lad?"

"Don't know yet, dear." Otto turned back toward the house. "Yeah. Stumbled up to the house 'bout noon and conked out right there in the yard. Poor boy. He's been fading in and out all day. Keeps going on about some countess's goons clobbering him and his friend in camp."

Addya leaned closer. "He's likely one of the ones the watcher sent to track Countess Yarek, which causes these feathers to wonder if the courier got through."

Karl nodded. "May I come in and see the lad?"

"Yes, of course." He waved them in and turned

in toward the door. "Drew! Take care of the sheriff's horse."

A boy of about fifteen darted out. His short hair blew in the wind.

Karl passed the reins to the boy and grabbed the saddle bags. "Thank you."

He led Addya to the house. The man stood aside and gestured them in. A savory smell lingered.

The back wall had a couple alcoves closed off by curtains. The fireplace was set between them. A lidded pot hung on a hook, near the fireplace. A small wooden table had four stools. The lady of the house, Elsa most likely, sat on one. Her floor-length gray tunic was belted at the waist. Her brown hair hung loose around her shoulders. Her arms were wrapped around the neck of a shaggy, hip-high dog with a black and white pelt. The dog strained against the woman's embrace. A long, fluffy tail swept back and forth while the dog panted.

On the opposite end of the room, a straw pallet had been assembled with a blanket laid over it. A young man lay facing the wall. A cloth had been tightly wrapped around his chest and shoulder, and a blanket covered him to the chest.

Karl gave Addya the saddle bags, rushed over, and knelt next to the young man. "Johann." He turned back to the owners of the house. "You say he staggered up to your house and collapsed?"

Otto nodded and walked over. "That he did. Had a couple little crossbow bolts stuck in him, not much longer than my hand. Sent for the physician in town. He says the lad can't be moved for a while, but he should be fine if the wounds don't turn foul."

Addya's talons tapped on the wooden floor as she approached. "We should divide. You find out where the other tracker is. If he is also injured, he needs you. I'll continue alone."

"No need for that, miss." Elsa sniffled. "The boy, Johann was it? He said his friend was killed."

His parents will be devastated. Their youngest. Karl fished a few of his larger denomination coins from his pouch, clasped Otto's wrist, and folded the coins into his hand. "To cover Johann's expenses and your efforts to care for him until he can travel again. I'll stop by on my way back and cover any additional cost. If he's still here, I'll take him home."

Otto turned the coins over in his hand. "Thank you, sir, but I don't think it'll come to this much."

"Keep it for now in case it does."

The boy came in and closed the door after him. "The horse is settled. I threw a blanket over him."

"Thank you." Karl reclaimed the saddlebags from Addya. "May Addya and I shelter in your stable?"

"Out there?" Otto aimed his thumb toward the back corner of the house. "Warmer here, sir, if you don't mind the floor."

Addya stepped forward. "We intend an early start and would not want to wake the house."

The boy rolled his eyes. "That won't be a problem. Up before the sun here."

"Teer sleeps with Drew, so the dog won't pester you." Elsa ruffled the dog's shaggy head.

Karl set the saddlebags near the wall. "Thank you. We appreciate your hospitality."

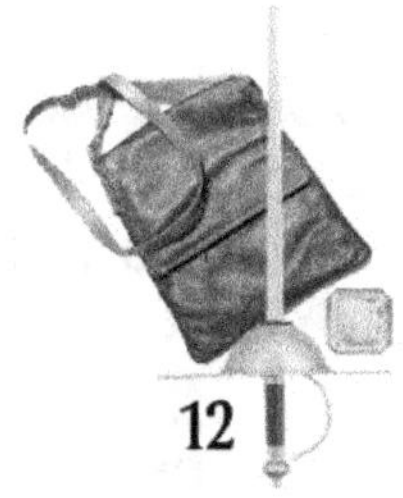

12

The repetitive thud-crack brought Addya from a sound rest. She opened her eyes while keeping her beak tucked under her wing. The light in the small cottage suggested dawn had come within the last hour or so.

So much for an early start. She hissed and rose, catching the thin, patchwork quilt she had been given last night. The dull pain in her head surged forward again, and she winced. *That can stop any time now.*

The lady of the house sat at the table chopping up root vegetables and dumping them in a pot simmering on the fire. A spool of dark thread and a heavy needle perched on the other end of the table.

Clothing repair and cooking? You've had a busy morning.

Elsa smiled and continued her food preparation. "Good morning, miss. Sleep well?"

Too well. "Yes, thank you." Addya folded the quilt and placed it on the spot of the floor that had served as her bed.

She crouched next to Johann, who somehow stayed asleep through the thud-crack coming from outside. His chest rose and fell with a slight wheezing noise.

"The sheriff already changed the bandages on

the boy's wounds." Elsa nodded toward the sounds coming from outside. "He said to let you sleep, but you should get him once you wake up. The menfolk are outside doing the chores. Sure you can't stay at least until breakfast?"

"Your offer is generous. Sadly, we cannot. We have a critical errand to finish." Addya slipped her tunic on and secured the buttons.

She stepped outside and tugged the door closed. Addya fluffed out her feathers. There was no wind this morning, but the air was cold enough without it. Following the noise around to the side of the house, she found Karl chopping firewood. Well past him, Otto dragged a tree from the nearest bit of woods.

Karl paused and nodded. "Good morning."

The axe descended and split the wood with a thud-crack.

"You let these feathers rest too long." She stopped a few strides from where he chopped wood.

"You do have a head injury, Addya. The rest will help your recovery." He split another chunk of wood.

"I will rest when the errand is finished."

He set the axe aside and dusted himself off. "All right. Let's take leave of our hosts and get on the way."

She followed him back inside and paid her respects to Elsa. Then she took their saddlebags to the barn and readied Pferd while Karl helped Otto drag the tree into the yard. Once everything was ready, They bid the family farewell and set out.

When they crested the third hill, Addya took one last glance back at the farmhouse where Reiker's man lay after being ambushed. "There is no way to know if the rider got through to Count Quetik."

Karl nodded. "I know. I've been thinking about that. We also don't know whether the caravan master was in on the plot against you, so he may or may not deliver the message given to him. On the other hand, if Countess Yarek attacked our people headed north, then very likely, the messenger headed west to the capital will travel safely, at least as far as her troops are concerned. He should get there tomorrow at the earliest. Count Quetik is in danger and may or may not receive word in time. I think we should head there first. Deliver the warning to him so he can be prepared then turn toward the capital."

"You intend to continue with these feathers out of Schafland?" Addya asked.

"Unless that would cause problems, yes, I think th–"

Low-pitched barks were cut short by a screechy yelp. A woman screamed.

Addya spun toward the farm house. "Go. I will arrive as quickly as I can."

Pferd and Karl galloped past her. She ran up the hill and launched from the crest, spreading her wings to catch the air. When she lost too much velocity to glide, she landed with a jolt that reminded her of the still-healing head injury. She ran up the next hill and launched off again. A human black powder gun popped then banged in quick succession. As she ran up the third hill, she drew the small crossbow and pulled the string back until it clicked into position. As she pushed off from the top of the final hill, she had a clear view of the house. A group of humans swarmed the house. One was already down. Another staggered away from the fight. Otto stood between his family and the men, swinging a scythe at anyone who came near. The dog stood nearby with his teeth bared, hackles raised, and one forepaw curled up toward his chest. Karl arrived at the near edge of the fight and stayed on horseback, slashing attackers with his sword.

She landed near the base of the hill and ran at an angle, coming at the group from behind. As she drew near the battle, she nocked a bolt. The nearest man charged at her, and she fired. The bolt caught him in the chest a couple finger-widths away from his sternum. The bolt sank to the fletching. The human staggered to a stop and fell flat.

Dead or not, you're finished with this fight.

She tucked the crossbow back into its place and drew her sword. An older man with graying hair and missing teeth spun toward her.

"This is foolish, old one." She settled into the half-crouched human fencing form, better for these melee situations.

He charged at her with a mace held high. Addya sighed and held her ground. She ducked under the first swing and grabbed his wrist with her open hand. Stepping in toward him, she drove the rapier's point through his rib cage and jerked her sword free.

Movement at the edge of her right vision drew her attention. Another man charged at her brandishing an ill-kept sword with spots of rust down the length of the blade. Less than two strides away, he raised the sword for an overhand chop. Addya hopped backwards, and the old blade swished through the space she'd occupied. She stepped in and grabbed the bell of the sword and wrenched his hand backwards while she pierced him with her rapier. He fell, and she kept his sword for her off hand.

Liable to come apart in my hand, but while it works...

Five remained. The dog had one pinned while Otto dealt with another. Karl was warding blows from two while the remaining ran around to flank him.

Addya screeched and charged toward the ones fighting Karl. One cocked back his arm to pummel Karl with a mace. Addya caught the goon's arm and yanked him backwards off balance. He hit the ground with a huff and struggled for his next breath. She slit his throat and ran after the flanking attacker, arriving in time to deflect the dagger descending toward Karl's hip.

Using the leverage of her blade's forte and bell, she shoved him away from Pferd and Karl.

"Strike unannounced?" She drilled him with narrowed eyes. "Such dishonor should startle these feathers. It does not. Very sad."

The attacker regained his feet and slinked forward. With only one opponent left, Addya straightened into her preferred style. She stood erect with her right side facing the man. Her right arm was extended with the blade aimed at his eye while the battered sword in her left hand was drawn back so the pommel almost touched her shoulder.

She fixed her sternest glare on him. "Show wisdom and leave this house with your life."

He froze and stared at her with wide, watery eyes. While he hyperventilated, Addya held her position.

Please leave. I've had enough death and destruction for one day and the sun is barely over the horizon.

He backed away then turned and ran.

She relaxed her guard. Karl finished his attacker about the time the dog tackled the one harassing Otto. The attacker threw the dog off and ran. Teer limped after him at a remarkable speed, but the man got away.

"What was that fight regarding?" Addya joined Karl and Otto at the door of the house.

Karl dismounted. "They're from the caravan."

Addya looked Karl over and found no obvious injury. "Then they were seeking these feathers and tracked us here." She shoved the point of the borrowed sword into the dirt. "Are you injured, Otto?"

"Not so it'd matter. Teer took a good whack on the foreleg when he got one of them away from Elsa, though."

"Let's get these bodies dealt with." Karl turned and clasped her arm. "I don't know if it'd be better for you to go on alone and I'll catch up or wait for me so we can travel together."

She fished a dingy cloth from her pouch and wiped her blade off before sheathing it. "As anxious as I feel to reach our destination, I would have great difficulty fighting ten at once." She gestured at all the bodies in the field. "I will assist here. The work goes faster this way." She grabbed the nearest body and pulled it toward the rocky terrain beyond the farmland while Otto tended to his family and dog.

Karl studied her then smiled. "You are different from what I expected."

"Have you not greeted other Aelstrians?" she asked.

"I think it was the first meeting that colored my view of your kind." He picked up the feet of the man she carried. "My family was affected by the last treaty."

"That was in an earlier year than I lived. How was your nest affected?"

They set the body down on the rocks and returned for another.

"We lost half our land and our home. The Aelstrian king paid us for the house and land, but I was maybe seven or eight at the time. Eight-year-olds don't understand these things."

That explains your caution. "Eight?" She laughed then recalled the longevity of humans.

"What?"

"These feathers have only ten years. I understand how losing the nest would devastate one so young, though. Grandfather's nest was also affected. He had to relocate to the other side of the river, as these feathers are told."

"I did not realize the treaty affected both Schaflanders and Aelstrians. Yet you've been just as concerned about Yarek's effects on us as you have your own people."

She snorted and set the second body down with the first. "Yes, well, holding anger after our ancestors' offense is neither fair nor wise, is it? Your watcher is old enough to witness those events with his own eyes. Not these feathers, and you were only a fledgling when the treaty changed the edge of the countries twenty years ago. That is a lot of years, and creatures change."

"I suppose."

"For whatever it is worth, these feathers also saw an effect. I lost an inheritance of social rank and land, but that is nothing against why you hurt for what occurred. I only lost a nest and a title I never knew. Losing a nest you know well is sad. For fledglings even worse. Let us finish our task or worse than lost nests will occur." She walked back with him to continue the grim chore.

13

The airship landed with a thud and a crunch of gravel in the courtyard at Count Zyrus Quetik's castle.

Countess Talia Yarek rose and wagged her finger at her guards. "You know what to do. Don't fail me."

Iado stretched himself out on the floor and moaned pathetically. The other guards picked him up and carried him out of the airship. Talia followed them.

Talia drew a deep breath and projected her voice. "Be careful with him. He's hurt badly enough already."

The courtyard was smaller than her own, hardly large enough to land an airship of any decent size. That would work to her advantage. Her massive craft would block the line of sight for most of the guards on the walls.

Green and gold banners hanging from the flagpoles along the walls fluttered in the breeze. Once her people were successful, those banners would be the first to go. Such a disgusting color arrangement would not last long in her control.

The count exited the main door of the keep. His black feathers were natural, evidenced by the slight variations of dark gray in his wings. Green beads decorated his crest and matched the tunic he wore.

The scales on his hands and lower legs were worn and wrinkled. Killing such an ancient specimen might be kinder than he deserved. Making him live out the rest of his existence in prison would be more fitting.

"What happened?" Quetik asked.

Talia rushed on ahead. "Oh, Zyrus, it was terrible. I sent my captain and a handful of others after a villain who crossed into Schafland. Trying to do them a favor, you see. When I didn't hear back from them, I tried to retrace their route, and I found this poor fellow half-dead. The only survivor! I wasn't sure he'd live long enough to get home. You were closest."

Iado moaned and his head lolled to one side.

Quetik squinted first at Iado then at Talia.

"Please, can you spare a room and a physician? I'll pay the expenses, of course."

"I'm sure that won't be necessary." Quetik opened the iron-braced oak door and gestured for her to enter. "Up the stairs to the second floor. First door left is a guest room. Set him down in there."

Talia led her guards into the marble-floored foyer. A carpeted grand staircase led up to the second floor then wound around to go up again. She lifted her long gown far enough to walk up the steps without landing beak-first and led the others up the stairs slowly to avoid winding herself.

At the second-floor landing, the countess directed her guards through the first door on the left and followed, closing it behind her. They set Iado on the bed.

Iado quit his pitiful moaning and propped

himself up on his elbows. "So, now what? He was supposed to follow us in here."

"At his age, I wonder if he can still handle the stairs." Talia clicked her beak and ruffled her feathers. "He'll be along, I'm sure. You keep playing your part until we have an opportunity to execute the next phase of the plan."

"Hopefully before Reiker's messengers arrive."

"They won't arrive." She stalked over to him and glared. "We took care of them on the way up."

"All of them? I'm not sure, and what about the courier?"

"Headed for the capital most likely, and if she does dare to show her beak here, we'll have control. I'll have those papers back, and she'll get a traitor's reward."

The door opened. Iado flopped back on the bed.

A tan-feathered male in a green tunic entered carrying a leather bag. "Good morning. I am Doctor Syriac."

"Where's Zyrus?" Talia clacked her beak and gave the doctor a narrow-eyed stare.

"Countess, your visit wasn't planned. You caught him in the middle of urgent business. He'll be along. In the meantime, I'll tend to your wounded one."

Talia nodded to one of her guards. He grabbed the doctor and hauled him backward, off balance, clamping an arm across the doctor's shoulders and a hand around his beak.

"Bind him and keep him quiet." She paced and crossed one arm across her chest. She propped her other elbow on her hand and tapped her beak with a long, decorated finger talon. *Is Quetik wise to the plan, or is that excuse honest?*

Either way, she needed to overthrow him quickly while she still had surprise on her side.

She pointed to two of the more able guards. "You and you. Come with me. The rest of you, fan out and tell everyone you find that the count has requested their presence in the audience chamber."

Talia strutted down the stairs and through the keep to Zyrus' study. Within, voices chattered, but the dense oak door obliterated the words. She knocked.

After a burst of hushing, the talking stopped.

"Enter," Zyrus said in his wheezy voice.

Talia threw open the door and plastered on her most benevolent face. The count's study was decorated in brass furnishings and green-cushioned furniture. His hideous wife stood next to him. Her splotchy, random cream-colored and tan feathers gave her the appearance of a mere peasant. The least she could have done was dye them all the same color. Her eyes were set far too close together, and one of them had turned the same shade as her paler feathers. The half-blind old biddy wasn't hardly worth the air she breathed, and that gown with the embroidered hem was months behind the current fashion. Ghastly.

"Zyrus, thank you for sending the physician." Talia entered and walked over to the elderly couple. "He's tending to my injured one now."

"Good." The count stepped forward and gestured to the two guards flanking Talia. "Did you really think you'd need protectors here?"

"That depends. What do you think of our current king?"

"We've already had this discussion at the capital and all opinions were made clear."

She squinted at him. "So you still approve of Evryt."

He snorted. "When the other choice is you? What do you think?"

"I think you have made an unwise choice." She backed away from the couple and tapped both of her guards on the arm. "Lock them in their own dungeon. Then once everyone is in the audience chamber, secure the exits. Then get that balloon out of sight, but keep it ready."

Addya led Karl almost due northward from the farmhouse. The countryside flew by but didn't change much. The hills of Haufenwache gave way to the hills of Count Quetik's territory in Aelstria. Even the frequency of the stunted shrubbery stayed the same.

The lingering headache had complained about the speed of their travel all day, but with Count and Countess Quetik possibly in Yarek's flight path, how could she move any slower?

A farmhouse in the distance glowed with candlelight in the oiled-paper windows. Squawks and chirps carried on the breeze.

Pferd trotted up next to her and matched her

speed.

Karl leaned closer. "So, we actually have crossed into Aelstria."

Addya launched off from the top of the hill and glided. "Hours ago. Early-afternoon at the latest."

"I've never been able to tell the border that clearly."

She glanced up at him. "If not for the house we were close to right around then, I would not know, either. Then of course, there's that ahead."

Addya glided to a landing and jogged to a stop. Count Quetik's castle sat on the crest of a hill. Trees around it had been cleared for a distance twice anyone's gliding range. The wall around the old castle had been built of white rock probably quarried up north and hauled down to the building site. Lookout towers stretched skyward at even distances all the way around, but from this distance, she couldn't see who manned them. The flagpoles were bereft of their usual green and gold banners, but then this close to sunset, they'd probably been removed for the night.

The lower walled area nearby was the city that supported the count and relied on his benevolent guidance. The garrison's own tower peeked above the city wall.

Karl reined Pferd in and stepped down. "Is that the place?"

We would stop here for another reason? "Yes."

"I wonder if she's here."

"Her craft would travel faster, and she had a head start. The question is, did she travel here or veer off to her allies for reinforcements?"

"We won't find out sitting here." Karl blew out a breath. "Let's go."

She followed him through the last of the scattered brush in the waning sunlight. Looking past Karl, she studied the castle walls. What was missing?

There should be more movement. Addya caught Karl's arm. "Wait."

"What's wrong?" Karl pivoted toward her.

"I see no one in the guard towers."

He squinted and studied the nearest tower. "That one's empty, which would be odd."

"We were not fast enough." Addya hissed and squinted into the dull light. "She arrived here already. I should never have gone with the caravan or waited the extra day. I could have gotten here first."

"That head injury would have gotten the better of you. I don't think you would have made it this far as quickly as we did, and there's no guarantee that you could have prevented this." He clapped a hand on her shoulder. "Anyway, it's too late now for those sorts of recriminations. Deal with the situation as it is. Would she have had enough time to reach her allies and send reinforcements to hold the castle?"

"No. That would have required an extra day or two with favorable wind in each direction." Addya ground her upper and lower beak together. "So, she has ten at the greatest: herself, the driver, a servant, and six or seven guards. As long as we encounter only a few at one time, we should do well."

"You would have us just walk in?" His eyes widened.

"How else?"

Karl pointed to the city. "Is there a garrison in that town?"

"Of course. Think your way through. Even if we convince the garrison leader that Count Quetik is in dire danger, do you think Yarek would hesitate to kill all the Aelstrians of that castle when her guards see the attacking force? All she would have to do is get all of the count's servants and household in one enclosed area and toss in a toxic grenade. All dead and we haven't crossed the gate yet. Alone or the two of us, we have a greater chance of defeating Yarek's retinue without getting Count Quetik's staff killed."

Karl blew out a breath. "True. I just wish we had more information going in."

"With the guard towers as they are, I can scale the wall. I doubt I will see anything. I can try, though."

He shook his head. "You might be spotted. If we're going to do it this way, the element of surprise is going to be necessary." Karl unhooked the knife from his belt and tucked it into his boot. "Along that line, hide a weapon somewhere."

Good idea. She clipped her own knife to the armhole of her tunic with the blade against her feathers. The extra bulk wasn't entirely comfortable, but it didn't impair her movement. Discomfort she could deal with. "Let us go."

After leaving Pferd in the care of the town's

stable, Addya led Karl to the gate of Count Quetik's castle.

She struck the metal-reinforced wood with the side of her scaled fist. "Open for the courier of the king."

Her heart thudded in an erratic march beat. Her muscles tensed, ready to leap or draw the sword at her hip.

Relax. Addya fluffed out and shook, releasing a pale, diffuse cloud of dust.

Karl sneezed.

She glanced over at him. "Sorry."

He rubbed his nose and grimaced. "Warn me next time."

The gate rose straight up with a creaking of chains, gears, and wood.

Once the gate was high enough to duck under, a lilting Aelstrian voice said, "Enter then, Courier."

Addya followed the human through. As she ducked through, she scooped up a handful of gravel. The gate dropped back into place with a bang.

A black-feathered Aelstrian with red beads in his crest stood next to the winch. This one belonged to Yarek. Any guard legitimately belonging to Quetik would have natural feathers and green crest beads.

The silver rapier in the guard's grip pointed at Addya. "Hand over your swords."

"That effort wasn't long-lived, now was it?" Karl mumbled and feigned struggling with the buckle on his sword belt.

We aren't done for yet, human. Addya reached for her own belt's buckle, but flung her fistful of gravel at the guard.

He flinched and backpedaled. Addya leapt toward him and caught his sword arm at the wrist. She pressed hard against the tendon at the base of his thumb. He hissed and dropped the blade. In a quick motion, she twisted his arm behind him and pushed him against the guardhouse wall.

"How many of you are here?" she asked in Aelstrian.

"Enough to take control of the castle," he answered through his clenched beak.

They hustled him into the guard house and secured him and his beak with the lacings of his own black tunic.

Addya walked toward the front door but only made a few strides.

Karl caught her by the arm. "No, around to the kitchen is best, I think. Stay close to the wall."

She shrugged and gestured for him to lead the way. Diffuse candlelight bled through the curtains of the count's study, but with the drapes closed they couldn't tell who was doing what in there. No lights showed in the rest of the castle windows.

Around the back, they came across the door. Clattering and banging of metal on metal and wood echoed from inside. Karl held up his open hand as he slowed to a stop and pressed his ear against the door. He held up one finger.

Addya drew her rapier. Karl gripped the hilt of his own sword. He flung open the door and charged in.

A heavy-set female in a stained apron squeaked and backed herself into a corner. She held her trembling fists close to her chest under her beak. Her tan-striped, brown feathers had red beads in the crest.

Another of Yarek's. Addya stepped past Karl and glared at the servant while speaking in Aelstrian. "Speak truly, and you'll be unharmed. What has become of Count Quetik's people?"

"In-in-in-in th-the audience chamber. C-countess Yarek is going to-to execute Quetik." She squeezed her eyes closed and turned her head away.

Addya closed the distance without advancing her blade. "When is this to happen?"

"Now, it-it-it may have-have even happened already!"

"What's the story?" Karl asked.

Addya mentally exchanged her language for his. "Yarek will execute Count Quetik in the large hall. It could occur even now. We go."

"Go. I'll render this one harmless and catch up."

She listened a moment at the kitchen door then flung it open and stepped aside. No bolts flew through. No red eyeshine beamed back at her from the dimly lit corridor.

She ran down the short, narrow hall until she reached the wider main corridor. Addya stopped and peeked both ways. Clear. She darted down the hall to Count Quetik's audience chamber. Light seeped under the door frame. Angry voices argued within. A loud slap preceded a woman's shriek.

Addya gripped the hilt of her rapier. She threw the door open and stepped in. The overhead chandeliers were lit, casting multiple, vague shadows around the room. Most of three dozen green-clad or beaded Aelstrians were sitting bound on the floor. Iado stood over one of the females with his hand poised to deliver a blow with a knife. Five of Yarek's guards stood around the room, and all but Iado had their small crossbows armed and aimed at her.

No sign of the count or his wife. The little vulture of a cook lied to us!

Iado pressed the point against the female's throat. "Surrender, Courier."

Even at her fastest, Addya could not dodge the crossbows and save the woman. She lowered the point of her rapier to the floor and let her blade fall.

"That's better." Iado speared one of the other guards with a hard gaze and twitched his head toward the front of the castle. "Get Countess Yarek."

The guard unloaded his small crossbow and darted out.

Iado clicked his beak. He shoved his hostage at the tiled floor and stalked toward Addya. "Did you think we wouldn't know you were coming? We had a lookout in the highest room of this place."

That should've occurred to me. "Of course, you did." Addya snorted and rolled her eyes. "We're not fledglings, Iado."

"Hand over the papers." He stopped well outside her reach.

"Get them yourself."

Iado's eyes narrowed as he looked her up and down. "You think I'm a fool."

As a matter of fact...

He pointed to one of the countess's guards. "Search her then bind her hands." Knife in hand, Iado stood over the same female he'd threatened earlier. "If you even flinch, Courier, she dies."

"Aren't you the brave one? I'm flattered that you think I could defeat all 5 of you at once." She held her arms away from her body.

The guard rifled her courier pouch and helped himself to her coin purse. The papers she had so carefully guarded were gone! Addya turned a startled gasp into a derisive snort aimed at Iado. Where were the papers? If Karl took them, she'd have to thank him later, after she skewered him for invading her pouch again. The guard took the knife she'd hidden in the armhole of her tunic before he bound her hands with a strip of cloth. When he tightened the cloth around her wrists, she winced.

The guard stepped away from her. "No papers."

Iado ground his bottom beak against the top one. "Where are they?"

She snorted. "I don't have them."

"You're lying."

Addya shrugged. "Your man couldn't find them, could he? They're not in the pouch, and this tunic has no pockets." *Karl had better have them.* She turned her head and lifted her crest feathers. "No, they're not there, either. Watcher Reiker sent several couriers with notes while I was with him. Perhaps the papers went with one of them."

He traded the knife for his sword and aimed at her. "You wouldn't have let them out of your sight."

"So you would think, and yet they're not here."

Iado pushed the other guard out of the way and pressed the sword's tip against Addya's throat. "Tell me where they are, Courier, or I will kill you and search your corpse."

Karl checked his knots then gave the cook a light tap on the beak. "You stay here now. We don't have it in mind to hurt servants unless we have to. Hmm?"

The cook quivered. Her brows knit together as he stood and backed away.

He retrieved his rapier from the table and hustled to the door leading into the hallway. No noise. Karl pressed his back against the wall and opened the door. After a quick peek, he crept down the long, dark corridor to the wider crossing hallway. His boots tapped on the hardwood floor in defiance of his efforts to move quietly.

A male Aelstrian voice chirped and whistled. Countess Yarek answered in the same language. The smattering of Aelstrian Karl knew gave him nothing useful to work with.

Don't suppose you could repeat that more slowly or, better yet, in Schaflandish. He stepped back against the wall and hid his rapier behind his leg.

The almost spherical countess strutted by with one of her guards. Karl stepped into the wider corridor and whistled.

The guard drew his sword and turned in a single movement. Karl beat his opponent's blade aside and drove the point of his rapier through the leather tunic below the guard's collarbone. The guard gurgled and sputtered as he collapsed.

Countess Yarek gasped and knelt next to the guard, leaning way over him.

Since when did you care so much for anyone but yourself? Karl kept a close eye on her. *Exactly what are you up to?* He tapped her shoulder with the flat of his blade. "Get up."

She grunted and stood, keeping her hands balled up in loose fists. "I should have known that Reiker would turn traitor on me. Where the courier was, I would have to find you, too."

"Not just us." Karl tipped his head toward the city. "We stopped in town before we came. They were a little surprised by what we had to say."

The countess snorted. "You should know this is fruitless. Even if you have alerted the town, we're well-entrenched here, and Iado has Addya in hand."

"I think you and I can change that." He pointed down the hall with his rapier. "Move."

With her beak held high, Countess Yarek turned and strutted down the hall. Karl followed.

When they neared the main door of the castle, something round and heavy hit the floor. The countess shrieked and ran out the door. A metal sphere rolled toward Karl and erupted in a rapidly growing cloud of gray-green smoke. He covered his mouth and nose and staggered back. A violent cough tore up the back of his throat. His muscles were weighted. His nose and lungs burned. Metal clattered on the hardwood floor.

Addya shifted away from the sword point pressing against her throat. "I told you, Iado, I don't have the papers. You understand your native tongue, don't you?"

A piercing shriek reverberated down the hall.

Iado rolled his eyes and slammed his rapier back into its sheath. "We finally get the courier in our talons, and the countess wants to flee?" He groaned.

Addya snickered. "Problem?" *What sort of mischief are you getting into Schaflander?*

"Let's go, Courier." He grabbed her arm in a firm grip and pushed her toward the hallway.

The other guards followed. Further down the corridor, between them and the main door, a gray-green cloud of smoke billowed. A man coughed vigorously. Could that be Karl? Something metal hit the floor moments before a muffled thud. Addya squinted, trying to find a shadow or a form in the midst of the fog.

Iado hissed and pointed down the hall away from the smoke. "This way."

She resisted the pull on her arm, still trying to catch a glimpse of the human.

"Get moving!" Iado yanked her arm.

Addya stumbled after him.

He directed his men through the next door and into a sitting room decorated in green velvet and gold. The scattering of well-padded chairs blended with the satin curtains. Books and games decorated the small tables ringing the room.

He punched the bell of his rapier through the glass window and swept away the shards remaining in the frame. "I'll go first." He shoved her into the arms of one of his guards. "Keep a good hold on her or lose your life." He stepped out through the window. "The courier next. The rest of you follow."

Addya sat on the windowsill and swung her legs around. Iado grabbed her by the arm and jerked her out of the opening. She landed hard and hissed.

Halfway to the gate, Countess Yarek waddled toward the opening at a speed Addya wouldn't have expected for one so large.

She scanned the courtyard. Could she pull free of Iado and run for it?

A sharp point pressed against her ribs.

Iado leaned closer. "The countess has been anxious to kill you, but that won't keep me from taking care of it if you try to break away."

The countess reached the gate and turned. She crossed her arms over her massive belly and glared at the guards.

I wonder. Will you actually consider freeing the one we have tied up in the guard house, or will you leave him behind to face the punishment for his part in your actions? Addya clicked her beak several times. "Does she even know how to operate the gate mechanism?"

"Be still, Courier. You've caused me enough problems." Iado nudged one of the others. "Open the gate."

The guard ran on ahead as the rest of them

picked up the pace. By the time they reached the gate, it was open. Muffled squawking came from the guardhouse, but the countess didn't spare a glance that way.

Once she was through the gate, Iado rolled his eyes and pointed to the guardhouse. "Get him, and be quick."

They continued on around the side of the castle wall where the red and black airship waited. The countess boarded as they arrived and parked her bulk on the only real chair in the place. Iado pressed the knife point against Addya's ribs and pushed her into the airship's basket, following close behind.

"Pilot, Lift off!" the countess screeched.

The airship rose. The remaining guards scrambled on board. The last jumped for it and hauled himself up. Except Iado, they all perched aft as the airship spiraled upward.

Countess Yarek held out her scaled hand palm up toward Iado.

He shook his head. "She says she doesn't have them. We've searched her, and there's no sign of the papers."

"Where are they, Courier?" The countess's eyes narrowed.

"Like he said. I don't have the papers." *And I wish I knew who did.* Addya clicked her beak. "My courier pouch was thoroughly checked. I have no pockets. Can't hide anything that large under feathers. I don't have them."

"Then you know where they are." The countess tensed.

"Well, actually, I don't know. Best I have is a

guess. My ally may have taken them. I tend to get into more trouble than he does."

The airship leveled and flew a straight course.

The countess preened the feathers above her right eye. "Then I have no use for you. Iado, throw her out."

Addya pulled at the cloth binding her hands. There was no stretch or play in the material. If she couldn't spread her wings, she'd fall like a rock.

Iado opened the basket's door. "My regards to your cousin when he meets up with you."

He gave her a shove.

She made a wild grab for the edge of the opening and missed, tumbling toward the sparse trees below.

Addya brought her hands up to her beak. She pierced the coarse material with the sharp point and bit down, twisting her head back and forth while pulling her hands apart. Her arm and neck muscles quivered. The hills came up at her too quickly. Her breathing sped up and her heartbeat was louder than the humans' black powder guns. The cloth ripped. Addya's head snapped toward her chest as her arms stretched out. The upward push of the air threatened to tear her arms off at the shoulder, but she caught the wind and arced away from the hills and toward the clouds.

She circled to get her bearings and willed her heart to a more natural rhythm. The wall of Count Quetik's castle was near enough she might actually land on it, but the count's people were most likely loose now. A jittery guard with good aim could end her trip to the capital. Addya turned parallel to the wall and glided to the ground. As her feet touched down, she stumbled forward and collapsed onto all fours.

Graceless. She squeezed her eyes closed and tried nothing more complicated than breathing. *Can't stay here. If they circle back to ensure I made a crater, I'll be pelted by crossbow bolts or worse.*

Addya pushed off from the ground and ran for the castle gate.

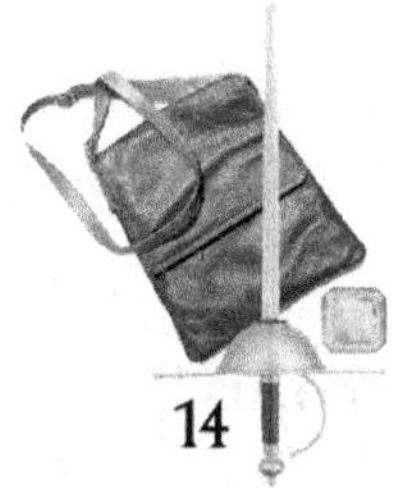

14

Squeaks, chirps, and twitters intruded into Karl's weariness. Bird songs were usually relaxing, but did they have to carry on so close to his window? His bed moved. It floated and bent around. When it finally settled again, it felt softer, but sunlight burned into his closed eyes. Karl groaned and turned away from the light. His body was too heavy, and his throat burned. Water would help that, but then he'd have to get up.

"Schaflander?" A firm hand gave his shoulder a shake. "Schaflander, are you well?"

The voice sounded older than the parchment used for the last treaty, but it was kind enough.

The bird chirps returned, clearly two voices this time. One was much higher in pitch than the other, which sounded like a heavily used reed.

Karl clenched his eyes closed a moment then squinted up at the biggest black and gray finch ever. Another massive white and tan mottled one stood behind him. These birds were big enough to be wearing actual clothing. One had a green tunic, and the other had a green gown.

Wait. Wake up, you fool. They're not outsized birds. Aelstrians.

"We were quite worried a'out you, Schaflander." The black one tapped Karl's chest. "You wear the syn'ol of our good friend. We thought you dead at first, and when we saw the grenade, well, what could we think?"

What are you talking about? "I don—" His voice croaked like a frog chorus.

The white and tan bird darted away then returned with a bowl of water.

The black one slid his hand under Karl's shoulder and pulled him up. The room swirled to the right.

Karl pressed his hand to his temple as the black bird tipped the bowl to Karl's lips. He sipped it and lost some down his chin. To avoid an unwanted bath, he took the bowl from the bird and finished the water himself. The twirly feeling in his head subsided some.

He set the bowl aside and took stock of his surroundings. The room was done in dark wood and brass with green cushions and tablecloths on every horizontal surface except the desk. He sat on a long, narrow couch under a wide window.

I should know who you two are. He set the empty bowl aside and studied the old male while the fog in his brain lifted. "Count Quetik?"

He nodded. "I a' indeed, and 'y wife, Celi."

Karl bowed his head. "I am Karl Schildmann, sheriff of Watcher Hans Reiker. I came with Royal Courier Addya Dace to warn you of Countess Yarek's plans before we turn for the capital. I'm afraid we were too late."

"A good effort, all the sa'e. Why go to the king?"

"Addya is carrying evidence of the plot. When our messengers to you turned up dead or beaten, we turned north first."

Pushing off from the couch, Quetik paced away and back again. "Then Talia 'ust act now 'efore she loses all advantage."

He crossed to a brass pull chain near the wall and gave it a few sharp tugs. The door slipped open moments later and a small Aelstrian with striped tan feathers tiptoed into the room and tipped her head down.

"Send for the 'ilitia captain." Quetik returned to pacing.

The little one left again.

"Where is Addya?" Karl asked.

Quetik spared a glance. "Servants tell 'e she had to yield to 'rotect a 'aid. Talia took her when they left."

"They'll kill her for not handing over the evidence." Karl bolted to his feet, making the room twirl.

Celi pushed him back into the couch.

Quetik returned. "Where would you go? You cannot fly, and they left 'y air."

A knock pounded on the door. Quetik chirped. The door opened, and a tan and black Aelstrian pushed Addya into the room. Her rapier and knife were both missing, and thin red streaks marred her wrists, but she carried herself with her usual confidence.

"Addya!"

He sat up, but Celi pressed her bony hand firmly on his shoulder. Quetik and Addya's escort twittered back and forth before the escort left. Addya came forward. Outside Quetik's arm reach, she knelt and bowed her head, fluffing out the feathers on the back of her neck.

"Rise, Courier. Your friend has told 'e a'out your efforts." Quetik offered Addya a hand up then inspected the marks on her wrists. "What is this?"

"The countess tossed these feathers out once they reached altitude. I had to free these hands, and I had little chance to use caution." Addya ran a scaled finger over the scratches. "I heal soon enough. You look well, Karl. I wondered if that was you in the gas cloud."

He managed a half smile and hoped that heat in his cheeks was not a blush. "It was. I should have known she was up to something when she became too concerned about her fallen guard. She threw you out of the airship?"

"Yes, when she learned you have the evidence. Where is it, anyway?"

Quetik preened his cheek. "You do not have it?"

She shook her head and patted her courier pouch. "No, I thought it was in here. It is not."

Won't you be surprised? Karl smiled. "This morning early, while you were sleeping, I had the farmwife split the lower hem of your tunic, insert the papers, and stitch everything back up."

She checked the hem. The new stitching was black against the dark brown of the tunic.

Quetik laughed. "Clever!"

"These feathers are less certain." She hissed and stared at Karl with narrowed eyes.

Karl held up his hand palm out. "You're a better fighter than I am. They would be safer with you, and you could still honestly say that you knew nothing of their whereabouts."

"A conflict to solve at another ti'e." Quetik brushed the dispute away with the wave of his hand. "What to do now?" He paced and tapped his beak with a finger talon.

"The countess will surely recruit her allies." Addya glanced toward the city. "If I can suggest, collect your own forces. I can continue to the king and seek his aid."

"Yes, yes. I have already sent for the 'ilitia ca'tain. I could use your hel' here. Your skill is well known. Others could carry word to the king." Quetik stopped and turned to Karl. "Reiker knows this threat, then?"

Karl nodded. "He knows, sir, and he's already sending word to the rest of Schafland to prepare for invasion in case the countess either bypasses you or breaks through."

Addya looked first toward the capital then back toward the east. "If I go, I should leave soon. If I stay, the other courier should leave soon."

Quetik shook his head and pointed at the window. "It is too late in the day."

"I have traveled at night on other occasions."

"Only under the greatest need." Karl watched the last arc of the sun dropped below the horizon. "Our previous night travels would have been unwise if that caravan hadn't been plotting our demise."

"This is a great need." She pointed over her shoulder with her thumb. "Do you think the countess will delay for us?"

Quetik made a slicing motion with his hand. "I will not allow it. Dawn at the earliest."

Addya's beak ground together then she fluffed out her feathers and shook. "As you say."

"Yes, I know you are anxious to finish your duties." Quetik crossed to her and clapped her shoulder. "The king will understand your delay. He is not at risk. We are in 'eril out here, and I have sufficient resources to resist a siege for a long ti'e."

Karl pushed himself up. When Celi tried to pin him down again, he patted her scaled hand and rose, ducking out of her reach.

"The countess may not return here at all, actually." His vision danced to the right, but he blinked hard and pushed his way past the unsteadiness. "She's lost any element of surprise with you. I think she'll try for someone still loyal to the king but unaware."

"Or she could try Schafland." Addya preened some errant feathers on her arm. "She holds your kind in great disdain. I do not think she would care that your lord already knows the danger."

"What about the count north of here?" Karl asked.

Addya waved the idea away with her hand. "One of the countess' allies."

"That one?" Quetik's eyes widened. "You are not serious. He can hardly tell his 'eak from his talons."

"There were insulting words next to his signature on the evidence. Nevertheless, he is one of hers."

Karl ran his fingers through his hair. "Then it'll be here, Haufenwache Fold or Bewachen Fold in the far south, and the first two much more likely than the third if she took off to the north."

"Then here it is. You two fly to the ca'ital at first light to get reinforcements." Quetik tugged on the brass chain a few times.

Celi chirped and twittered while she hustled over to Addya and corralled her in a one-armed embrace. The door opened. The countess led the courier out as another young page trotted in.

Quetik gave his instructions then gestured Karl out ahead of him. "Let us see what serves for dinner tonight then see what 'rovisions you will need."

Karl stepped out through door then stood aside to allow the count ahead of him.

Talia Yarek clicked her beak once as the balloon settled in the courtyard of Duke Dartin Lixine. The pilot had apparently understood her request to improve his landings. Her honor guard lined up at the door and proceeded to announce her presence. Once they finished, Iado followed her out and under the sword arch into the moonlit courtyard while Dartin watched from the window of his keep.

Can't even be bothered to come greet me? You'll learn better manners soon!

A guard clad in gray and white met her and conducted her to the duke's study.

Dartin perched on a gray-cushioned chair and gestured to another one. "It's late, Countess."

"Are you ready?" She planted herself in the offered chair, which creaked ominously.

"Ready? For wh—Now? We're starting the revolt now? What happened to 'be ready in a month?'" He leaned forward and jabbed his taloned finger at her. "This has to do with the message about the courier 'traitor,' doesn't it? What exactly did Evryt's agent steal from you, anyway?"

Talia cleared the air with a swipe of her hand. "It doesn't matter. What matters is that this is the time to move. Send word to Azel, and let's get moving. My people are already on the way to the rendezvous."

"Yes, I sent as many units as I had prepared already. I had a feeling you wouldn't wait an entire month." Dartin strode behind the desk in the corner and tugged a pull chain. "Let's get the rest going, and I suppose you'll be wanting dinner and lodging tonight as well."

Talia snorted. "You can manage that much, I'm sure."

She glared at the duke and kept a hard eye on him while he gave instructions to the servant who answered his summons. For the moment, he was useful, but as soon as he was not, she might have to kill him, too.

Addya smoothed out the blue tunic she had borrowed from Countess Celi's handmaid. After preening a few displaced feathers, Addya adjusted the rapier at her side and tucked the evidence retrieved from the old, leather tunic into her courier pouch, turned right side out again. She tossed her cloak around her shoulders and fastened it before darting down the stairs to the ground floor and out into the courtyard. The morning air chilled her, and she fluffed out her feathers. The sun hadn't risen yet, but there was enough light to discern shapes and obvious colors. An airship in green and gold sat in the middle of the courtyard. This one, only half the size of Countess Yarek's aerial behemoth, fit easily within the walls of the castle grounds. Zyrus and Celi Quetik stood nearby. A wicker handbasket hung from Celi's arm.

The door opened behind Addya, and Karl entered her peripheral vision.

He drew his cloak tighter around him and lifted the hood. "Chilly this morning."

"Colder aloft. Are you ready for this?" She waited for him.

"I'm with you."

Celi and Quetik met them partway.

The countess offered the basket and spoke in their native language. "Food for your journey."

"Thank you. We appreciate your hospitality." In deference to the Schaflander, Addya changed to his tongue. "If the king is willing, we will return as soon as we have delivered the evidence."

"Travel safely. I will watch for your return," Quetik said.

Addya boarded the small airship, then waited for Karl to get situated before she chirped take-off instructions to the pilot. Below, Quetik chirped orders to his people, telling them to open the armory, and get the townspeople armed and ready for a siege.

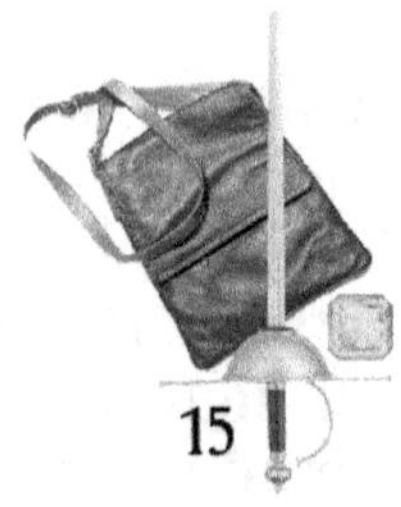

15

Addya peeked through the view port over Karl's shoulder. The great, walled city had been built in oak trees tall enough to touch clouds. Blue and silver flags flew on masts stretching above even the greatest trees. Other banners were hung from the branches. Through the heavy foliage, spots of other bright colors were visible. Addya found the pale green of her home and fencing school.

Thoughts of sleeping in her own bed, even for just one night, made her yawn. "It is good to return to the nest. We will arrive soon."

Karl turned toward her. "You live in this city?"

"Yes. It's hard to find the nest at this angle if you do not know what you seek. I will show you if there is a chance. I should see how the fencing students have done while these feathers were away. I get the idea I will have to leave for a while again."

Karl let the view port flop closed. "The sun's just now over our heads. We might be back on our way this afternoon."

Addya returned to the bench. "That will hinge on whether Evryt sends us to Quetik alone or with a force, and whether or not he has a force collected already. I dislike the idea of leaving Count Quetik, or Watcher Reiker, without aid for long."

"Don't try to take so much onto your shoulders.

You can't be in both places at once."

"Yes, and I had duties to the king while Quetik could very easily come under attack." She got up and paced the length of the basket, barely two of her long strides.

"He's warned and prepared." Karl sat on the bench in the center and watched. "If the king already had his suspicions when he sent you out, then a prudent leader would already be equipping his men."

"You are right." She perched on the bench next to him and preened while the pilot maneuvered the airship into position for a landing.

Crosswinds buffeted the air ship, pushing it off course. As the pilot came back around for another attempt, Addya hissed and went to the window.

I can glide from here and stop wasting time. She glanced back at Karl. *Be patient. Stop acting like a fledgling on Hatch Day.* She sat next to the Schaflander until the pilot landed the airship and declared they were safe to disembark.

Addya opened the door and stepped out. Evryt and Jianna stood at the edge of the platform with a retinue of guards.

Evryt's feathers were a shade or two darker gray than Addya's. His nearly black crest had sapphires and silver for decoration. He stood a full hand-length shorter and was dressed in blue-trimmed white. Jianna had chosen a gown that matched her husband. The diamonds and sapphires in her dark brown crest sparkled in the sun. As usual, not a single feather was out of place.

Jianna rushed forward. Addya met her halfway

and tucked her beak to her chest.

"I was so worried," Jianna chirped as she preened Addya's neck. "I wish he wouldn't send you on these more dangerous ones."

Addya stepped back. "I asked for it, and it was fortunate that he agreed. I needed every sword skill I own."

"So Gavril tells us." Jianna led her back to Evryt.

"How is he?" Addya asked. "Chal wouldn't let me try to help him."

"He is safe among us and recovering, but he is finished as a safe house operator in Yarekia. After leaving Gavril here with us, Chal left for home immediately." Evryt whistled.

Addya knelt, but Evryt caught her arm and pulled her up.

He leaned closer. "You found something?"

She produced the evidence and handed it to him. "Plenty. She is amassing an army now to march on either Count Quetik or Watcher Reiker. Both are alerted. They'll need reinforcements."

"I can't send a force to Reiker. Schafland would perceive it as an act of war without a representative requesting help." Evryt looked past her. "Oh, you've brought one of them with you."

Karl's boots clacked on the wooden platform. Addya stepped aside and pivoted to clear the way. Karl stopped outside arm's reach of the king and knelt.

Addya spoke the human language. "I introduce to you Karl Schild'ann, a sheriff of Watcher Hans Reiker. He has served with these feathers as a great ally."

"Then you are 'ost welco'e." Jianna lifted her hand palm up.

Evryt looked beyond them at the airship. "You certainly left Quetik when dawn was not fully hatched to arrive at this hour. We shall eat our lunch and set our strategies."

The king escorted his wife down the ramp toward the tree canopy. Addya gestured Karl ahead of her and followed with the retinue of guards taking their positions behind her.

Karl inspected the tiny bolts for Addya's miniature crossbow. They were fine as far as he knew, but his weapon of choice was his pistol. He knew little more about crossbow bolts than how to tell one end from the other. None of them showed any cracks. They were all straight. The feathers were smooth, and the pointy ends were pointy. He handed over the money Addya had given him to pay for the bolts then picked up the leather bag they were in and squatted next to the reddish-brown Aelstrian page she had assigned to guide him.

The page tipped his head to one side. "Done?"

He nodded once. "Done."

"Next?" the page asked.

"Addya's School."

"Follow!"

The page's Schaflandish was actually pretty good for one so small, even if he tended toward monosyllabic queries and responses.

Just like the trip to the bowyer, the page darted on ahead to the next intersection and waited until Karl caught up. Although no less anxious than the page, Karl kept his pace slow enough to observe the treetop city around him. Aelstrians in various colors of feathers and tunics glided between the platforms built into the trees or walked along the bridges. Feather dyes were apparently more popular than he realized. In addition to the usual browns, grays, and tans of natural Aelstrian coloring, many had taken on hues not found outside of cloth dye vats. The colors extended to the buildings themselves. The walls were painted in impossibly brilliant hues.

The Aelstrians gave him plenty of space, many darting into a building's doorway until he'd passed. Many of them showed more fear than hostility, and the royal messenger sash Addya had given him brought more than a few stares. He smiled or tipped his hat as he passed them.

They reached Addya's school. The page reached the door first and clutched the doorknob.

"Gently." The page opened the door slowly and led the way in.

The front room of the school was a large, open area. A cluster of four adult Aelstrians perched in a circle on the floor in the center of the room with a collection of papers spread out in the midst of them. They chirped and whistled in turns, pointing to things on the papers.

Addya held up one hand to pause the discussion. "Very good, Havi. Thank you for guiding Karl. Very good use of the door. You can return to the steward now."

The little page tucked his beak to his chest for a moment then bolted out, slamming the door behind him. "Gently!" the page yelled. He opened the door then closed it soundlessly.

Addya snorted. "He is learning. We are nearly finished here, Karl."

Karl nodded and found a spot to sit and look around the room. Baskets lined up along one wall, probably for personal belongings of the students. Above them, posters showed pictures of armed Aelstrians in different poses with writing in the swirls and wedges of the Aelstrian language. The model in the picture bore a remarkable resemblance to Addya. The desk in the far corner had neatly stacked papers, quill pens, and ink bottles. Practice swords, daggers, cloaks, and bucklers hung in a rack on the wall opposite the baskets.

After a few more minutes, Addya gathered up the papers as all four Aelstrians stood. The three other adults bowed their heads to Addya before they left. She piled the papers in a neat stack on the desk and joined Karl as he stood.

He handed her the pouch. "They looked good to me, but I don't know much about arrows and bolts, I'm afraid."

"These feathers are certain the arrows are fine." She shook one into her hand and inspected it. "Thank you for retrieving the arrows. Any difficulties on the way?"

Karl shook his head. "Lots of stares, but no problems."

"Good. Let us go or we will arrive late."

He followed her out of the school and down various connected walkways. Unlike the page, Addya walked with him. Fewer stares came his way, and many heads bowed as they passed. Addya bowed her head in answer.

The wide steps up to the castle were decorated with banners in the king's colors. Glass ornaments shaped like birds and butterflies hung in the treetops and cast colored splotches on the steps and banister. The guards at the main gate admitted Addya and Karl without question. Beyond a short foyer area, the throne room opened up with a balcony ringing three sides around a lower veranda. The fourth side was a raised dais on which gold nests were decorated with blue cushions.

Addya led the way down a flight of stairs to the floor of the throne room then across to the wall opposite the dais. She reached behind a tapestry, and a slender door clicked and opened in what appeared to have been an empty part of the wall. After pulling the door open, she gestured him in ahead of her.

The room inside had a large table with a map of the continent. Aelstria was mapped out in various colors matching the heraldry of the various landed nobility. Schafland was a variety of grays. The king was there along with a few other stern Aelstrians who wore black doublets decorated with medals in the royal colors. Addya introduced him to each of the generals, but a few seconds later, he forgot all but their rank.

"Good, you arrive." Evryt spoke Schaflandish for Karl's sake and gestured for them to come closer.

"We discuss what forces we have and where to send."

"To Quetik, of course," the nearest general insisted. He pointed to the green section of the map. "The attacking forces have to go around his territory to get to Schafland, and we do not need Schafland thinking we want to attack."

Karl shook his head. "My Watcher has alerted the rest of the nobility about the threat from Yarek."

"Exactly. Forgive these feathers for saying so, Schaflander, yet several of your kind see all of our kind as having no differences.

Evryt leaned over the map and pointed. "If we can halt the attack here, we can save the Schaflanders who live in outlying areas."

A carved blue gem glittered on the ring gracing Evryt's long finger.

Karl stared at the large stone.

"What is it, Karl?" Addya asked.

"That gemstone. I have one much like it. Payment to my father for our land in the last treaty. The symbol carved in it is different but it's about that shape, though somewhat larger. I hadn't seen one like that anywhere else."

The king studied his ring for a moment. "You are fortunate indeed. Few are given. The stone grants you the status as a friend of the throne. That grants you royal favor."

"Interesting, however, not what we need," a general with tan-striped brown feathers said. "Our forces are gathered all to the east and north. We need only to collect the forces in our craft and head to Quetik."

"At first light," the nearest general said.

"You wish to add a thought, Addya?" Evryt leaned toward her.

Karl turned toward her and saw the same squint in her eyes that he'd seen while trying to convince her to stay in Haufenwache after her injury.

Addya tapped her finger talons on the tabletop. "He will have a siege to deal with if we wait until first light."

"Can't avoid that, Courier." The nearest general clicked his beak and snorted. "We are no good to Quetik or anyone else if we leave without true readiness."

The third general at the table, an older one with graying feathers, cleared his throat. "I have served with Quetik. He can fight if need 'e. The situation is not ideal, 'ut he can hold off the likes of Yarek and Dartin. That's no fledgling they are dealing with." He punctuated his words by stabbing the air with a weathered talon. "Flying at night just gets us off course and lost. I' sure of that, Courier."

Addya nodded once. "I do not doubt you, sir. I only worry for those I left in danger."

"You did your duty, Courier. No one can ask 'ore than that."

Evryt stood up straighter and adjusted his doublet. "First light, generals. 'E underway as soon as the sun rises enough to travel safely."

With heads bowed, the other Aelstrians present fluffed up their head feathers until the king had left the room. Then the generals left. Once they were alone, Addya blew a hard breath out through her nares.

"You don't like their solution?" Karl turned his

back to the map and leaned on the table.

"It is good sense; however, I would have wanted a quicker return. It was the duty of these feathers to deliver the request for assistance and the evidence of Yarek's treason. It is also true that I fight effectively with one or only a few targets. These feathers are likely useless in a siege. I do not think in those kinds of strategies and tactics. Still we go to Quetik again, and I still think I have a fight with Iado to consider." She blew a breath out through her nares. "I hate this. I would rather fight Iado than leave the fight to one with less training, though." She stood and straightened her doublet much like Evryt had done. "Do not concern yourself for these feathers, Karl. As you noticed in Haufenwache, I worry too often."

Karl accompanied Addya out of the hidden room and back to her school.

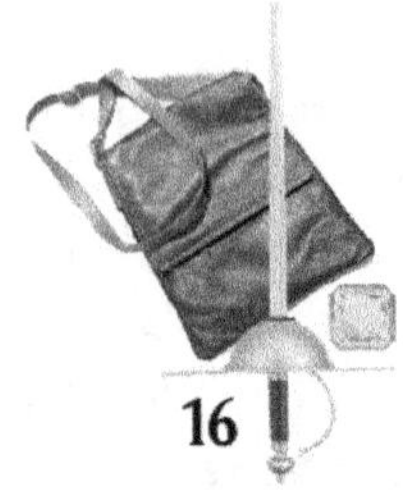

16

Count Zyrus Quetik lowered the hand shielding his eyes from the dawn sun as he stepped away from the window of the corner tower. Troops bearing black and red banners took up positions inside the trees to the south and west. Another force in gray and white came in from the east, and a third with orange banners came down from the north. Balloons in each of the colors of the attacking armies sat on the ground inflated for take-off or hovered above their respective forces waiting for the signal to attack. There wasn't enough space in his courtyard or in the city proper to inflate and launch more than one or two dirigibles at once, which only made them good for target practice. His archers and arbalests would be earning their keep today if they warded off the balloons.

A group of three Aelstrians approached, stopping beyond arrow range. One representative came from each of the three attacking armies, and Yarek's bore the flag of truce.

"Here comes the ultimatum. Might as well hear them out," Quetik muttered.

He hobbled to the balcony facing his courtyard and stepped off. His wings caught the air and he drifted down in no particular hurry. The representatives wouldn't go anywhere until their message was delivered.

Once he touched down at ground level, Quetik headed for the stairs leading to the crenellations on the outer wall.

An archer met him.

Quetik held up his hand. "I know. I saw them from the tower. Be a good girl and help an old man up the stairs."

The archer leant her arm.

His old knees protested and creaked as he moved, but he made it to the top and leaned on the crenellations. "Well? What do you want? I don't have all day."

The flag-bearer stepped forward and whistled the message. The shrill pitch didn't carry well enough for his old ears. When the garbled squawking quit, he turned to the archer who'd helped him up the stairs.

"What was that?"

The archer leaned closer. "We were told to surrender, or there will be no quarter."

He snorted. "They would not have given us quarter in any case." He held his hand toward her. "Crossbow."

She passed it to him.

"Bolt." He drew one from her quiver and nocked it.

He estimated the range, aimed, and fired. The bolt landed short enough that it posed no threat to the truce flag but close enough that it delivered his response adequately.

Quetik handed the crossbow back to the archer. "Eyes bright, archer. Reinforcements are coming by nightfall at the latest, I'd say. We'll hold out that long at least."

Karl stared out of the view port flap. A flotilla of blue airships surrounded the lone green one borrowed from Count Quetik. Other than the crew, he and Addya had this airship to themselves, but the rest of the ships in the fleet each carried a contingent of the king's elite soldiers, each with their own commander. One general was along to coordinate them. A second general remained in the capital to oversee the defenses of the castle if necessary, and the third general was off to the north to collect the forces of any trustworthy allies.

After letting the flap close, Karl sat on the bench and rested his elbow on his knee and his chin on his palm. The novelty of airship travel had worn off. At least the sun was well overhead now, and the early morning chill had fled.

Addya perched on the bench. "Not fond of flying?"

"Hm?" He startled and sat straighter. "Oh, it's fine, I'm sure. Like you, I want to end this soon, but I want it to end well. There are a lot of farm houses and small ranches scattered around the countryside in Haufenwache. There won't be time for the people to retreat to the main cities, and even then, the smaller cities won't have sufficient defenses to hold off an army."

"Likewise, there are outliers around the

Aelstrian countryside. That is a hazard of living off alone." She gripped his shoulder. "If we are not tardy, we can intercede."

"Will the commander of the reinforcements agree to that?"

"Those were Evryt's final instructions this morning. He does not want such a great quantity of civilian casualties, either. The general agreed, if we can get far enough ahead of our foes to get organized correctly."

A trill carried on the wind.

Addya darted to the eastern view port and rolled the flap up. She pointed. "There!"

Karl joined her. A roiling black mass raced across the ground below in the wake of a red and black airship. Red banners flew at the front, gray at the center, and orange at the rear. A second group came from the east bearing white and gray banners. Nearer at hand, Quetik's castle was surrounded by banners and troops.

He bit his lip. "Countess Yarek is red. The two with her are the count north of Quetik and..."

"The one northeast of Quetik." She tipped her beak toward the eastern group. "That's the duke."

"For or against us?"

"Against." Addya clacked her beak. "Evryt's hen had a clutch with another sire. Naturally the duke thinks Evryt cheated his way to the throne. Organizing against two fronts will require strategy. We have an insufficient quantity of fighters until our own reinforcements arrive."

Karl pushed on Addya's shoulder, turning her toward him. "Grenades dropped from this height will even the odds or put them in our favor, both around the castle and in the approaching army."

Addya shook her head. "And the unfortunate Aelstrians who did not choose to join the soldiers?"

"The gas grenades like the one that incapacitated me are no fun to be sure, but they'd incapacitate the bulk of the force, wouldn't they?"

Her eyes widened. "A worthy idea, Schaflander. If we can eliminate a large fraction of the force, Talia would consider surrender. Without her, there are no others so arrogant."

Addya leaned her head out the view port. She whistled and chirped.

Once Addya finished her message, she pulled her head back inside. Karl strained to hear the response. Addya preened.

The whistles and chirps were faint, and then there were others from nearer then further away. Finally, the same voice that had trilled at first answered.

Addya's eyes widened. "They like your idea; however, it will need all the grenades they have. The flock will divide and attack the different groups. It is for us to follow Countess Yarek and force her down. If all goes well, the flock will chase the individual traitors, and the general will return to us and arrest the countess."

Karl clapped his hands once and rubbed them together. "Excellent."

"What is the effective range on your gun?" She drew out her crossbow and slid the back off.

A group of small bolts dropped into her hand.

He drew his pistol and checked the frizzen and

the flint, careful to keep the barrel pointed away from Addya and his finger away from the trigger. "You're thinking to force her down by compromising the balloon?"

"Exactly. This craft is not large enough to shove her down."

"Fifty yards, perhaps. I have—" He opened his cartridge pouch and counted. "—ten shots."

Addya squinted at the far side of the basket for a moment then nodded. "I have a half-dozen shots with this." She held up the mini-crossbow. "If that does not convince her to land, I'll have to glide over there and try a direct suggestion."

He caught her hand and turned her palm up, revealing the scratches. "I don't like that idea."

"These feathers are not overjoyed, either. Nevertheless, she cannot get away." She clapped his shoulder and nodded to the nearest view port before she darted to the aft one and flipped it up.

Karl loaded his pistol and secured the covering with the strap at the top of the window. Blue airships dispersed. Two headed for the eastern force and three others headed for the siege while the other seven flew over the main group. The terrain ahead of the armies turned rocky, cut through with ravines and ridges. Countess Yarek's red and black airship grew larger, but the pilot of their own craft stayed well above the enemy.

Gray-green smoke clouds erupted on the ground. The roiling black masses stuttered to a stop. Addya's little crossbow clacked. Karl took aim at the countess' dirigible and fired. The powder in the priming pan flared and popped before the main charge blew. Addya had shot two more bolts before he'd reloaded and fired his second. She'd sent her last by the time he'd fired his third. Heated air shimmered as it leaked out through the holes.

She held up her hand. "Wait."

The red and black airship turned southeast but lost altitude as it fled.

"Now we just follow our target until they land." She joined him. "Leave Iado to me."

Oh? Karl cocked an eyebrow. "Revenge?"

She squinted and ruffled her feathers. "He is the reason Evryt sent me after the data."

Karl thought back to their other encounters with Yarek's guard captain. "He hasn't seemed all that formidable."

Addya held up her crossbow. "You shot one of these out of his hand and injured those feathers. He has healed enough now to turn into a hazard again. You say I have greater skill than yours, and I tell you that it is not certain these feathers can defeat his."

He nodded. "I understand." *I have more shots left. You may not have to fight him.*

Addya's borrowed airship settled into a depression among the hills. She gripped her rapier. As soon as the airship set down, she hopped out the open door. Karl's footsteps crunched the dry grass and rocks behind her. Overhead, one of the king's airships slowly spiraled toward the ground.

Some twenty yards away on the crest of a hill, Countess Yarek's balloon sagged. The gondola door stood open already.

She kept her eyes glued to the basket and turned toward Karl. "There was the countess, Iado, six other guards, and the crew of two or three. Watch yourself."

"Five other guards. I killed one before the gas grenade got me," Karl said.

"Right."

She led the way forward. *Come now, Iado. This is silly. Make this a straight fight and be done with it. Better yet, surrender.* She screeched in her own language, "Iado, come into the open and face me."

"Come get me, Courier," Iado shrieked back.

She pointed, directing Karl to try flanking the group from the left. She crept forward but stopped. Waiting at the bottom of the ravine for the enemy to show his beak over the ridge was exactly how she'd beaten Iado's band before. Falling for her own gambit would be foolishness of the highest order. She headed around to the right and scooped up a couple rocks. Addya pitched them toward the center of the ridge.

The steep wall of the ravine continued for yards before she reached a shallow spot. In the distance, the snap-bang of Karl's gun echoed off the stone.

You should have let me get in position, Schaflander!

Addya slid down the embankment into the ravine. All but one of Talia Yarek's guards raced away from her and toward Karl. The last lay sprawled on the ground with his hand pressed hard to his chest. Addya ran through the ravine. She had to get to Karl. Even she would have trouble against so many at once. At least the stone walls of the ravine were hardly a wingspan apart where Karl was. Flanking him in that narrow space would be harder.

Karl reloaded his pistol and took aim at Iado for the second time. Some twenty yards in the distance, Addya flattened herself against the ravine wall until he'd pulled the trigger. The sulfuric smell of the gunpowder and scorched, gritty taste wrinkled his nose. Again, Iado dropped into the dirt, and another guard fell. Karl cast aside the pistol and took up his rapier. His guts tightened. If there were doubts Addya could win against Iado, Karl didn't stand half a chance. With his two misses, he had Yarek's guard captain and three others to contend with.

I should have waited for Addya.

She was practically flying down the ravine. If he focused purely on defense, he might survive.

The first of the enemies came within range. The guard struck the erect, straight-armed pose of their favored style, one that didn't suit these tight spaces. Karl settled into the half-crouched human style and waited. The guard chirped and whistled.

"If you think I understand you ..." Karl smirked and shook his head. "It's probably a good thing I don't."

He waited. In a handful of seconds, Addya would

reach the back of the group.

Iado pushed his way past and adopted the human style. His chirping had a snarl built into it.

Karl gripped his rapier tighter and swallowed. *Defend. Just defend.*

Iado swatted at Karl's rapier, knocked it aside, and thrust at Karl's head. He snapped his blade back online and parried the blow over his shoulder. Iado twittered again before he beat aside Karl's sword and thrust. The point of the sword came closer to Karl before he could deflect the effort aside.

Try that trick again? He watched Iado for a sign of movement.

Iado drew back. When he tried to pop Karl's sword away, Karl dipped his blade lower and brought it up on the other side then parried hard.

The guard captain clucked and leapt to the attack. Karl hopped backwards. A rock shifted under his boot when he landed. He kept his feet but stumbled. Iado came on like stampede. Karl deflected an incoming attack upward. Iado drew back and drove in another thrust. Karl swept his blade aside but missed Iado's sword. Karl backpedaled but not fast enough. The sword hit his doublet. He twisted away from it, and the point dragged across the leather, leaving a deep score.

Iado stepped back and clucked. He threw a series of reflex-fast strikes. Karl parried the first two by divine intervention alone. The next sliced across his upper arm. The fourth pierced his leg. Sharp pain blazed from the wounds. He fell and switched his sword to his uninjured hand, a process complicated by an increasing tremor. His breathing came in sharp gasps.

As Iado drew back his sword for a strike, he laughed.

Addya held her opponent's wrist, stepped in and delivered the fatal slice across the throat.

That's the last. Only Iado and the countess now.

Further down the ravine, Karl fell. Growing blood stains marred his clothes. His labored breathing was as rough as the shaking in his hands.

Iado towered over the fallen Schaflander and laughed.

Addya picked up a rock and threw it, striking Iado in the lower back. She ran forward.

Iado hissed. "Yield, Courier, or your human pet will die."

"Because you are too cowardly to face an opponent of your own caliber?" She slowed to a stop an arm's length out of Iado's range. "Turn around. Try to strike him, and you'll die where you stand."

Iado turned toward her and closed the gap. "Go back to your school. You belong with the children."

"It's not that kind of school."

She settled into the human's stance and waited.

Iado pressed her blade aside and leapt forward. Addya jumped backward, freeing her blade and clearing the range of his attack. She drifted a few more steps back, and Iado kept pace.

That's it. Just keep coming toward me and

away from Karl.

Once she had a double handful of yards between them and her fallen ally, Addya planted her back foot. She beat Iado's blade aside. He disengaged under her effort then whacked her blade aside and kicked her in the gut. She staggered back a couple steps and pressed her open hand to her belly.

So much for an honorable duel. Am I surprised?

He pursued her. Addya deflected his blade high. He tried for another kick. She caught his leg and shoved him back. He landed hard on the rocky ground.

"On your feet, traitor." Addya stepped back from him.

He rose up into a crouch.

Go ahead. Take a leap at me from that position. Please. She tightened her hold on her rapier.

Iado hissed and stood. "You should have killed me when you had the chance. It'll be your own code of honor that destroys you."

"So you say."

His free hand was balled up at his side.

Rocks? Dirt? What do you have there?

She kept his off-hand in her peripheral vision and threw a feint. As soon as he drew that hand back, she leapt tailward. Dirt clouded the air and gravel clattered on the ground at her feet.

She clicked her beak a few times.

They traded attacks, parries, and counters with neither getting the upper hand. Addya's breathing whistled through her nares.

Iado jumped toward the edge of the ravine, kicked off and propelled himself into a somersault over her head. She whacked his sword aside as he landed and thrust at his shoulder. He parried easily.

He panted through his open beak. Iado shrieked and launched himself at her. She dropped into a crouch and thrust her blade at his belly. The sword drove through his leather doublet and out the back. He fell on her driving her back on the rocks. She curled forward to keep her head from smashing into the rough stone.

Addya grunted and shoved Iado off of her. She withdrew her sword and pushed herself up. "You were the better fighter, Iado. You just became impatient."

Karl sat where she'd left him. Blood leaked through the fingers clasped around his upper arm and across his thigh.

She jogged back to him, collecting his pistol along the way, and knelt next to him. "What did I tell you. Leave Iado to these feathers?" She spoke his language.

"I thought I could shoot him from a distance. He ducked both times!" Karl rolled his eyes. "Are you all right?"

Addya nodded. "How are your injuries?"

"Hurts. One might need a surgeon."

"I will find cloth to dress your wounds."

"Courier?" The general's chirps carried to her easily.

"Here, General, in the ravine," she answered.

Steps came closer and the general's off-white crest plumage appeared before his face. "I was going to see if you need help, but you have all in your talons."

"Actually, the Schaflander was injured." Addya stood and walked a few steps closer to the general. "I will need help dressing the injuries and returning him to the airship."

"I'll send our unit's physician."

"The countess?"

"She was not with her guards?" The general shielded his eyes with his hand and searched beyond the ravine.

Addya leapt for the ravine wall. "She cannot get away!"

With a hand on the rock, she stopped and looked back at Karl, and then at the general. There were few of her people beyond nobility and couriers who could speak the Schafland tongue. Catching the countess would have to rest on the wings of others.

The general nodded once. "We'll get her." He turned away.

She returned to Karl. "Aid arrives soon."

"The countess? You–" He tried to sit up but grimaced fell back.

"Not all tasks fall to these feathers. You need someone to translate for the doctor."

He managed a smile. "Thanks."

Talia Yarek hustled through the brush and trees. Branches caught her long dress, marring the beautiful beadwork and embroidery.

If I ever get my talons on Iado again...

Instead of protecting her, he'd suddenly decided to be more interested in his own feathers. Behind her, a human's pistol fired two shots spaced some distance apart and shrieks and whistles carried on the wind. If Iado had any luck at all, the king's forces would capture and kill him. They would be so much nicer about his death than she planned to be.

She huffed and puffed, trying hard to get enough air. Her muscles ached. She leaned against a tree, rubbing a sharp pain in her side. After a minute or two to catch her breath, she pushed off and continued on her way. The tree cover thinned to scraggly shrubs and knee-high grasses.

A loud trill came from overhead. She turned her gaze toward the balloon. The door swung open and soldiers leapt out, spiraling down on their outstretched wings.

Talia hissed. She turned away from the balloon and ran. The shadows of the soldiers crossed over her and in front of her, no matter which way she turned. A couple landed in front of her. She turned and found two more behind her.

A fifth one—wearing the ribbons that marked him for a general—touched down within arm's reach and grabbed her arm in a fierce grip. "Countess Talia Yarek, you are under arrest on charges of conspiracy and treason. Any effort to escape will be considered an admission of guilt and result in immediate execution."

She tried to shrug away from his firm grip. "Get your hands off me. You have no right—"

"Let's go, Countess. You can register your complaint with the king in the capital."

17

On the second morning after the short-lived battle, Addya finished making her rounds, and set the now empty water pitcher on the table at the edge of the throne room turned hospital ward. There were many injured, but most were on the mend. She had one more stop before she had time to rest her own tail. She ran up the stairs, taking two at a time, and tapped her talons on the door of the guest room where Karl had been resting.

"Enter," Count Quetik called in the Schaflander's language.

She slipped into the room and found Karl sitting up in bed with the count perched nearby. His color had returned. He wore a sleeping tunic and had the blanket tugged up to his waist.

Addya approached the bed, bowed her head, and fluffed out her feathers to acknowledge the count.

"You really should not. You outrank these feathers," Quetik said.

"These feathers are a courier. Nothing else."

"You are the correct heir. Your line is the correct one. Even Evret knows this, and with Yarek out of the way, he can surrender the crown to you."

Addya's stomach threatened a revolt. *Me? On the throne? I wouldn't know the first thing.* "You talk treason, sir."

"I talk sense. Without the threat of Yarek taking the throne, there are those who will consider revolting to ensure the correct lineage is restored."

"You talk of the twins."

"Yes, and others as well."

"A civil war would be tragic." Karl grimaced and sat up straighter.

Addya walked to the window and stared out at the workers who still hustled around cleaning up and repairing after the short siege. "At least let these feathers talk to Evryt first. He is the cousin of these feathers, and his wife is a friend."

Quetik gripped her shoulder. "You have a chance to think and talk to wise counsel as you take your new friend safely to his nest." He gestured to Karl. "I received word today. Watcher Reiker wishes his sheriff's return, and I offered your services in that direction."

She turned away from the window. "Of course. Can you ride, Karl?"

Karl gripped his injured leg. "The doctor advised that I not ride quite yet. Pferd would not appreciate a ride in a balloon, but he can draw a cart or travois. That is if you don't mind the trip."

"The weather is good. I have no issues with traveling in good weather, and Haufenwache is not too far aside from the way to the nest of these feathers." Addya grabbed Karl's mended and laundered clothes hanging nearby and handed them to him. "I will ready Pferd for the journey. You ready yourself. We will leave then."

Addya sat side-saddle on Pferd's back while the gelding pulled a triangular, wood-and-rope travois bearing his usual rider. Reiker's castle had been on the horizon this morning, and in minutes, the gate guard would be demanding her identity.

She twisted around toward Karl. "Nearly there."

"Good." He grunted and shifted positions. "This frame is becoming a permanent part of my backside."

"After such a quantity of days, no need to guess why."

A human guard came out of the gate and met them. "What is your business here?"

Addya reined Pferd in.

"Marc, it's me." Karl grunted as he pushed himself up. "Addya is a royal courier helping me get my pitiful self home."

Marc darted to the travois. "Sheriff! What happened?"

"Overmatched in a sword fight. Only alive as a result of the courier's timely intervention."

"Should I send someone to tell Watcher Reiker you've returned?"

"That would be best. He's not one for surprises."

The guard ushered them through the gate. As Addya directed Pferd toward the front of the keep, Marc flagged down a young boy and sent him on ahead.

At the front door, Addya tugged Pferd's reins

and hopped down. "We are here."

Karl grimaced and scooted closer to the edge of the travois. Addya offered her hand and pulled him up. He held onto her for another moment or two then hobbled forward on his own.

She kept his pace and watched in case he needed help. "You are getting healthier."

The door opened and Reiker came out onto the porch.

"Another day or two, and I think I'll be walking with just a bit of a limp." His jaw clenched as he stepped forward on his injured leg.

"Try not to take lots of days at once, or does such advice only work for anxious couriers?" she looked at him from the corner of her eye.

He smiled. "No comment."

The watcher held the door open. "You've been tended by a physician?"

Addya stepped back to let the humans walk together. "Yes, in the field and at Count Quetik's castle."

When they entered the narrow hall leading to the study, Karl used the wall for support. "I was ordered to put no undue strain on the leg or the arm for a week. A little over-cautious I think."

"Better that than the other option." Reiker darted ahead and opened the study door. "Please, come and sit down, both of you. You're just in time for tea."

The room hadn't changed at all. The same sparse, utilitarian furnishings and wall-length windows decorated the space without even the addition of dust.

Addya walked with Karl to the table and chairs near the desk and waited until he was situated before she turned a chair sideways and sat.

"Johann?" Karl winced as he shifted his weight. "When we stopped at the farmhouse, they told us he'd left already."

"He arrived last night, got a sound tongue-lashing from the physician for not waiting until he was better mended, then went home to rest." The watcher joined them with a small tray bearing a couple cups of steaming brown liquid and a bowl of water. "So, what is the state of things?"

She let Karl bring Reiker up to date with the events since their departure from the caravan.

"So, that's where it is now." Karl sipped from his cup. "Countess Yarek is in custody, the conscripted soldiers are being returned home if they'll swear their allegiance to the king, and the rest of the traitors are being rounded up by the king's elite division."

"What of the power vacuum in those regions? If you're not careful, you may end up with someone worse than you removed?" Reiker plunked a small, cubical sugar rock into his drink and stirred it.

"There are agents of the king in each of the cities." Addya preened the feathers on her arm. "The leaders of those agents will take control until a trusted lord or lady can ascend the throne."

"Better than martial law, I suppose."

A timid knock tapped the door.

Reiker sat straighter. "Enter."

A young boy stepped into the room. "There's another bird courier here, sir."

"'Aelstrian courier,' lad, not 'bird courier.' Show the courier in. Thank you."

The boy stepped back out into the hall. "Go on in."

Addya twisted around as Rava, Havi's older brother, walked in. Like the little page back in the capital, Rava's royal blue tunic clashed outrageously with his reddish-brown feathers.

"Here you are, Addya, and only my second stop." He rushed over and produced a note. "From the king, for you," he chirped.

Addya's eyes narrowed at him as she took the paper and spoke the human language. "Schaflandish, Rava, or you insult our hosts."

"Sorry. I' still new at this."

Reiker smiled. "That's fine, lad. What's the word?"

"The king wishes to know if all is well."

"Indeed it is. My sheriff tells me the invading army was stopped well within Aelstrian territory. My people were not at risk. He has my gratitude for his quick action."

Addya opened the note while the courier continued talking to the Schaflanders.

My dearest Addya,

Word has reached me that my loyal servant, Chal, has taken his final flight. I grieve for his departure. He had concerns about his flock. One may have alerted the guards to you and Gavril. He wasn't sure which yet, but he had suspicions.

Addya formed a mental image of the old bird who'd sheltered her the night she'd escaped and then had gotten her safely out of the city the following morning. He had been a venerable, old age for certain. His departure would be mourned, but if anyone had earned eternal rest, he certainly had.

It's just as well. Yarekia – which I suggest you rename – should be restored as the capital city. I will meet you there. As I promised my father, I need to restore the throne to your family line to preserve the peace within the kingdom and between us and Schafland. I know you aren't keen on this, but it must be done. My apologies. The school will continue in your honor. I already spoke to the other teachers, and they intend to continue your tradition unchanged. Jianna already misses you, but we will visit often.

Your cousin,
Evryt

Addya folded up the note and tucked it into her courier pouch. Apparently, she was going to assume her inherited title whether she wanted it or not. Father's lectures of duty echoed well from her childhood.

Eyes bright, Courier. There's a job to be done, and you're the only one who can do it.

"Anyway, I' glad all worked out well, and I have

delivered the note. I go now. Okay?" The courier bowed then retreated.

Once the door had closed, Reiker snorted and shook his head. "That one needs a bit more practice."

Addya nodded. "Your tolerance is valued. Others would have his head."

"We all start somewhere."

"Favorable news?" Karl tapped the paper.

She tapped her pouch. "No, another task for these feathers. The cousin of these feathers agrees with the northern count. The coronation will follow shortly in the original seat of the Aelstrian throne. What grieves these feathers even greater is the loss of a new friend."

"Oh?" Reiker finished his drink.

"The agent who assisted these feathers after I found evidence of Yarek's treason. He was aged and has gone to a larger, cozier nest."

"Ah, well, that is sad news and joyous news all in one message. From what I've seen, you'll make a fine queen, with a little practice and some good advisors." He nodded to the door. "The lad wouldn't stay, but you, you must enjoy my hospitality tonight, and we'll send you off in the morning." He planted his hands on the table then stood up. "Perhaps with an ambassador to make your further sojourn less disagreeable?"

Addya stood and offered Karl her hand up. "You would have the gratitude of these feathers."

"Sheriff?"

Karl accepted her help and grimaced as he stood. "I think that could be arranged. I can't resume my duties here for a while yet."

"At least until those injuries heal themselves properly, I think." Reiker smiled and nodded. "Well. Let's join my lovely wife in a more comfortable room and enjoy some conversation and perhaps some music. Shall we?"

Epilogue

Addya launched off of the platform across from the dais and glided over the heads of the gathered nobility and visitors of two countries. The month since her return to the proper Aelstrian capital had been spent restoring order and figuring out which of the guards and staff were decent people working for an evil taskmaster and which were servants of their former master. The coronation itself was formally correct even if it lacked the excessive decoration and frippery. The oath, the food and drink, and the guests were all part of the ceremony, but she had not found time to recruit entertainment. Just as well. The simplicity suited her better.

As she landed on the dais, a serving girl rushed forward and helped her tie the skirt of her gown on. The girl darted away, and Addya stood alone on the dais looking out over the crowd. Karl, standing to her left at the foot of the dais, leaned on his cane and smiled. The large, etched sapphire that his father had received as payment for his family's land formed the center of a brooch pinning a gray and black brocade cloak together.

The words of the oath fled from her thoughts.

She drew a deep breath. *All oaths start the same.* "I swear–" The words tumbled out as if connected to one another. "–to uphold the laws of

Aelstria, setting aside my personal objectives for the service of the people, to rule them in the best interests of the nation, to encourage peace and friendship with our neighbors, and to preserve Aelstria for all fledglings."

Originally from Michigan, Cindy Koepp combined a love of pedagogy and ecology into a 14-year career as an elementary science specialist. After teaching four-footers (that's height, not leg count), she pursued a Master's in Adult Learning with a specialization in Performance Improvement. Her published works include science fiction and fantasy novels, a passel of short stories, and educator resources. When she isn't reading or writing, Cindy is currently working as a tech writer, hat collector, quilter, crafter, and crazy African Grey wrangler.